The Carpenter of Auguliere

Also by D. Wayne Dworsky

Touching the Sky (the book)
Touching the Sky (the CD)
The Teachers Always Write

The Carpenter of Auguliere

By
D. Wayne Dworsky

Published in the United States of America by Concrete Jungle Press
New York, NY

Printed in the United States of America

ISBN 0-9749048-2-1
978-0-9749048-2-5

LCCN 2006927194

www.concretejunglepress.com

Dedication

This book is for Nenita Dworsky.

She knew from where all
my stories originated.

Acknowledgements

Again I find myself at the mountaintop realizing how inefficient my sole efforts are to get here on my own. It is not the physical energy of my supporters, but rather the spiritual uplifting that has given me the fortitude to complete my tasks. I am indebted to all those whose contributions are acknowledged in the nature of the characters of Auguliere.

The Carpenter of Auguliere is a work of fiction. The location and characters are all invented by the author. Any resemblance to actual places or people of the scenes and characters in this story is purely coincidental.

The people of Auguliere came to me in a dream, challenged me to exhibit them in the context of this unique place and special time. I tried my best to keep the integrity of their message intact and get their story straight.

—D. Wayne Dworsky

Prologue

When the last rains fell in the lush, green valley, the winds calmed too. The sun only flickered back and forth between the cloud plumes as though it played a game over the jagged ridges on either side of the giant Sayan Mountains. The abundant ore contained in the mountains was long forgotten, and so, too were the people's spirits of this majestic landscape.

"Move your fool selves along," shouted a herdsman. An alert dog ran ahead of the flock, chasing the sheep, directing them to their corral. An angry shopkeeper emerged to scorn the herdsman. He stretched out his weathered arms in angry rage.

"You can't run those animals through the streets of our town." The herdsman turned around to acknowledge the shopkeeper, now standing out in the street, shaking his fist in defiance. The dog barked and advanced towards the shopkeeper. The canine forced him to retreat into his shop. Women stepped into the street, sinking in the mud that the carriages made. Ponies trotted by, flicking mud all around them.

One pony flicked a chunk of mud from one of its hooves directly in the face of a passerby. She stopped to wipe the muck from her brow, and revealed an annoyed face as she searched for a source. The shoddy wagon, meanwhile, disappeared onto another street. The muddied woman noticed the little herdsman hiding behind his flock, and returned to a more fitting demeanor.

"If I see you come by Fleet Street again with those horrible beasts, I shall have Vladimir fine you." The herdsman looked back with fear at the woman's noble expression.

"Woman!" the herdsman yelled. "You would be less offended if you took up your position inside your abode as you should, or as any woman should for that matter."

"Monster of the rue!" she shrieked. "I will have your kind incarcerated at once. Just wait till I see Mr. Robertson." Two others entered the street.

"Raisa, Raisa," consoled another shopkeeper, one who apparently knew the woman well. "Don't be so troubled by those creatures. Don't let disruption in our village detour your efforts as a woman of society. Think of their meat, think of the service he gives, think of his duty as a herdsman, and never feel troubled again."

"Think of your drunken tenant who never pays the landlord's rent. Think upon it quite often." She lifted her dress, gawking at the man with her lower jaw hanging in disgust, and pranced through the street, stepping gingerly among the grooves that huge wagon wheels had dug. An old-timer poked his head out of a window on Sycamore Lane, a street that, while adjoining Fleet Street, only pretended to be one of the vital parts of the community.

"All of you," the old man yammered, lifting his head up out of the window like a rooster. "Let it be known that you are all stabbing your neighbors in the back, whatever it is about which you quibble." Before he uttered another word, a woman's arm reached for him and pulled him back inside the sanctuary of their house as she closed the window.

Another man came along driving a pony-drawn cart. He climbed out and stood in the street among the others, admiring the red brick building where an odd woman sat stiffly, leering out of her window like a possum waiting for a scrap to fall on the ground. She had very distinctive features etched on her ancient face. She stared past the man at another man farther away, who staggered in the mud, raising a bottle for all to see. She vanished from the first man's sight.

"I know the word of that man on Sycamore Lane," the second man said. "Let him not be pulled away like so many years of a man's life. I object to the way certain people are treated and what they have to put up with in the name of order!" The man fell to the ground, letting his bottle strike a large stone at the base of the wooden walkway.

"Look at you," a respectable tradesman yelled, looking down at the slovenly being he noticed at his feet. "You are a disgrace to your village—look upon your own spirits and see what they have done to you!" The man raised his head and witnessed the blood dripping from his hand.

A large black buckboard pulled by a mule team rode through Fleet Street, stopping by the aspen trees in the market square. The driver stepped down and smacked his skinny black cane in the mud, splashing the muck everywhere. The sky rumbled with thunder and the clouds stayed dark, but they only yielded a few droplets of rain on the caked mud.

"Raisa," the man exclaimed, his face austere and smileless. "Whatever brings you to the center of our delightful town market? You wouldn't be shopping by any chance, would you?"

"You need not make inquiries of my whereabouts," Raisa proposed.

"I don't see a need for a defensive posture," he assured. "What new ornament adorns your visage?" He smiled with a devilish grin. The man tugged at his broad-rimmed hat and whipped his black cape around him.

"That is the manner in which you prefer to conduct your business," Raisa told him in honest conviction, "to instill a defensive attitude in each who cross your path." He stepped back up on the walkway and blinked his eyes as he turned away, waiting for a chance to leer back at her. He turned around again, as though he had acquired renewed strength.

"The shopkeepers know their place, the farmers are aware of their land, the herdsmen are aware of their flocks, and the craftsmen know their trade."

"The strength of one shrewd man is procured from a mystical source," Raisa bravely spoke up. The man raised his eyebrows and gaped at the woman, stepping forward, almost daring her to confront him again, but he stopped in the street and glanced up at the town clerk's office door.

The door swung out, letting a young man affix the sign outside that read "open." He scrubbed his boots on a mat and disappeared back inside.

After Raisa passed, the man from the buckboard stepped down into the gullies on Fleet Street, walking until he reached the cobblestones in the market square. Several people crossed his path and acknowledged him with a "Good mornin', Mr. Robertson." He only tipped his hat to the ladies and nodded to the men. After a time, he looked both up and down the street, and entered the office.

A red-bearded man paused on the cobblestones. He set a piece of machinery down where he stood. He looked at his reddened fingers that burned from holding the sharp heavy metal. He looked up at the man on the landing, who turned to acknowledge him.

"Good morning, Mr. Carloff." Mr. Roberston smiled and retired into his office, leaving the streets quiet again. Mr. Carloff left the square as though nothing unusual had happened there today.

Much later, the night of the new moon left a velvet, dark hue on the entire village, keeping the shopkeepers within the boundaries of their street displays. Agafon Carloff came out of his shop again and this time walked up to the man in the street, who still held onto his broken bottle, barely able to keep his head up.

"For over a year now," Agafon said to him, "I have watched the buildings of our village disintegrate before our eyes."

"You know how to wield a hammer and saw?" the man asked.

"Iakov's time is past," Agafon assured. "He shall never rebuild our village. Nothing short of a miracle will rebuild it."

"I am not in the miracle business," the man said, letting his head lay against the rock. And the street was silent again.

Chapter 1

Madeleine peeked between the garments on the clothesline, beyond the yard, and over the fence. She saw the familiar form of a skinny man wearing a black suit and top hat, who leered back at her with a sinister expression, causing her to withdraw her gaze. She glanced over her shoulder at the faltering crop, making her shiver.

"Why have you failed to pay me the three rubles you still owe from last month's taxes, young lady?" the man scolded with a mean snicker.

She tried to answer, but the words stuck in her vocal chords. She felt around in the ragged dress pocket, finding it empty, which sent her senses to a higher level of desperation. Reaching into the recesses of her mind, she groped for the wisdom to answer him, but only discovered memories of hatred and despair.

"The next month's taxes are almost due," he reprimanded, shaking his finger at her.

He harbored threats that made her tremble. She stood behind the gatepost as though it would protect her. Neighbors gawked out of their blurry windows to witness the commotion, making her feel self-conscious.

"I don't have the money, Mr. Robertson," Madeleine finally pleaded, looking back at her crop again. "I don't know how I'm going to get it." The tear that formed in one of her eyes blurred her vision.

"I don't care how you get it," the man growled, poking his straggly beard. "If you don't have it by nightfall, my dear, you'll be sharing your bed with the birds."

He swung his black cape over his skinny shoulder, pressed his hat down over his bushy-eyebrowed forehead, and vanished as rapidly as he appeared. Madeleine was left shivering in the gloom of the overcast in the early morning, wondering how she would manage the debt. She was not only troubled by the three rubles she owed, but she was also bothered by the fifty rubles of the next month's taxes that she would have to find a way to pay.

She returned to her shanty, feeling defeated. The short entranceway in her garden opened immediately into a family kitchen. A door on each side led to a separate bedroom; the door on the opposite side opened to the street. Her father, Iakov Knesnovich, lay tucked away in his room. A generation ago, Iakov would have confronted Mr. Robertson and stood his ground. The years, however, had invigorated Mr. Robertson and left Iakov an invalid.

"Who was that, my dear?" Iakov called from his bed when she came into the house.

"No one, father," Madeleine said. He lay quietly on his back in the oppression of the sunless room. Only chirping birds interrupted. Otherwise, the valley was quiet. Her mother's death and her sisters living out of the house forced Madeleine to deal with her predicament alone.

"I heard you talking to someone from across the yard."

"It's not your concern, father," she said, composing herself. She came into the room and approached the bed, brushing her drooping, faded dress with her hands. She smiled in his presence just as her mother used to do, and placed her soft, fair hand on his perspiring forehead while he shivered under the blanket in the morning chill.

"Just rest, father," she said. "I shall take care of him." She pulled away, looking back, tossing her long, brown hair, regarding her father with a kind face. He remained in his bed.

"Did the crop sell well at the market?" he asked, making his voice echo to the next room. She stood by her hearth, looking straight at him through the open doorway.

"Yes, father," she said, swallowing hard, "we sold all our yield." She put her hand to her sticky cheek and left the room, to return to her own room.

"That's good, child," she heard him say faintly. "I heard Mr. Robertson went to the village this morning to collect taxes." Madeleine remained silent in her room, letting Mr. Robertson's unusual face pervade her mind. "I'm glad we got the crop out because the milkman said Mr. Robertson is imposing new water restrictions starting immediately."

The image of the drought-stricken corn smoldered in her mind. She sat on her bed, recalling the dust smell from the fields. She remembered how the pelting rain lifted the smell from the dust when it hit the ground. That was long ago when the husks were still green and the tassels danced in the wind. Madeleine walked to the table in the kitchen without answering, sat down and began to cry.

The village was nestled in a big valley with giant, sloping meadows, discouraging visitors. The valley was a place where the cattle sang as they grazed in the pastures. Ponies whinnied all day as they pulled carts for vendors who never smiled. Workers were consumed with worry. Women worked in the fields, corrals or chicken coops, in a constant state of gloom.

An enormous well occupied the center of the village, where all the cobblestone streets converged. Boys carried wooden buckets to and from the well daily. The old people never budged from their rockers, and the children played stone and stick games in the dirt. Egg collectors carried baskets of eggs to the market for sale. Some delivered eggs to people in their shanties. Milkmen delivered dairy products to shanties and shops. The town bustled with life, but it was a feigned life. Villagers greeted each other in monotone and they performed their daily chores in mechanical motion.

When Madeleine visited her old friend around the corner, she found an unexpected and unpleasant surprise waiting for her. No sooner had they sat at the table and begun exchanging greetings when the big knocker sounded. Madeleine's friend approached the door with trepidation. Her little son clung to her legs. Madeleine shrank back when she recognized the skinny figure at the door.

"Have you the taxes you owe?" Mr. Robertson said to the friend in a hurried voice.

"I have one ruble," the woman said.

"One ruble!" he screamed. "I thought I made it clear you must pay up all the money you owe by the end of the month."

"It's not the end yet."

"Don't test me, woman! I have seen enough of your kind. You owe me 150 rubles for three months' back taxes." He stood erect like a wooden soldier at the door.

"I am working as hard as I can for a widow with a child."

"I don't care about your marital status," he said. "The next time I visit, you must have the money." He executed an abrupt turn and walked away.

Madeleine understood how frightening the confrontation was even though she kept her tax bill almost up to date. The friend's son hid behind his mother, peeking out at the departing man from between her knees. Madeleine knew many others who shared the same fate. Several women were also widows with young children.

"I shall return at the end of the month," he called from the street.

Robert Auguliere, a fabled pioneer, had founded the village in the valley generations ago. It was a far-off place in a forgotten time, with ancient, weather-beaten buildings. The wood had dried, cracked, and splintered from years of exposure. Winds blew drafts through the structures and the shanties leaked from the rain. Most of the streets were unpaved, allowing the wagons that rode on them to carve deep gullies in the mud.

Mr. Robertson lived high up on the west hill near the alpine meadows, all alone in a large house. His grandfather had financed every structure in the village. When he died, he left all the real estate to his son, Robert junior, who passed it on to his son, whom he named Robert Robertson the third. Robert Robertson's wife died during childbirth of their only son. This heir remained anonymous and lived with his aunt Raisa. Meanwhile, Mr. Robertson III became monarch over the land. He inherited most of the property. On what he owned, he collected rent; on what was left, he collected taxes. He forever assumed the role of administrator, and supervised the county clerk. Consequently, the town people referred to Mr. Robertson as the property owner, or simply, "the landlord." The clerk was the only one besides the landlord who really knew how to run the village. He kept the records of the town straight and the landlord relied on him to carry out all the legal proceedings properly and maintain order.

The giant well, which occupied the center of a market, stood between two parks. The market always clamored with people. Seldom did anyone ever stroll through the parks even though they were adorned with dozens of aspen trees. Instead, people hurried to and from the market or huddled by their fireplaces and kept to themselves or their families. The children remained in their shanties and maintained morose expressions much of the time. Since electricity hadn't reached the village, everyone stopped working at night, sitting in shanties lit by oil lamps or candlelight. The women knit while the men smoked their pipes. There was nothing else to do except sleep until the next morning.

Around the village, the land sloped up to meet the alpine barrens where the goats wandered and the marmots played. They were the only creatures truly free. Ponies and cattle were constantly corralled. Shepherds took herds up the sloping meadows each morning, but returned them by dusk. People never wandered up the slopes alone. Ominous creatures patrolled these regions, making the area dangerous for individuals. The villagers remained subjects of this place and forever in its shadow.

Madeleine ran a small produce farm. Each morning she gathered eggs from her row of coops, collected produce from her land, and sold her goods at the market. This year the drought, however, left her crop without yield. Her father contributed less each year as the population continued to shrink. Over the years, he grew weary with age and withered away to a sequestered state. Madeleine thought he was giving up on life because he always had a new ailment, making her feel depressed. Some days she couldn't bear to see him so debilitated.

She still had dreams, though. She often wondered what she would do if he died. She was tall, young and often dreamed of a husband. She didn't want to be a farmer's wife. She wanted to leave the village and see what lay beyond the mountains. She needed to find out how other people of the world lived and what they looked like. There was no hope for her here. Each afternoon she sat by the window and watched her crops deteriorate under the veil of the forever-overcast valley.

In the late afternoon, after Madeleine had returned to her shanty, she sat in the kitchen watching the birds fly through the open window of her father's shop. As the sound of the knocker startled her, she lurched forward with concern, fearing the landlord had returned. When she opened the big oak door, the broad shoulders of a tall man appeared at her eye level. She looked up to see a red-bearded man. His face blossomed with a wonderful smile. For a moment, she felt vindicated, and saved from the horrors developing in her mind.

"Agafon," she said. "How nice of you to come." The red hair stood out against the whiteness of his face like blood on cotton. His presence made her tremble with excitement.

"I brought you some feed for your chickens," Agafon said, reaching for the sack without taking his eyes from her face. "You look upset. Whatever is wrong?" She led him into the kitchen, where he sat. She walked to her hearth.

"I'm sorry. I have just finished moving my father. You know how difficult it is to move a sleeping man?" She picked up the kettle, filled it with water, and placed it on the hearth.

"Does he sleep all day?" Agafon said, toying with his wiry hair.

"Almost," Madeleine said. "He's sleeping now." She poked the glowing charcoal and stuffed the hearth with fresh kindling.

"You will see Vladimir soon," Agafon said.

"He's coming here?" Madeleine said.

"Yes, he is."

"He is the mental strength of my life and you are the physical strength." Agafon blushed so deeply it was difficult for her to see his red beard.

"I am?" he asked with a gesture, making her giggle. "If my wife doesn't mind."

She jumped up with excitement and hugged him, with the poker still in her hand.

"Both of you are important men in my life," she said, pulling away and laying the poker down, realizing it must have seemed offensive even though Agafon had not reacted to it.

"What's that for?" he asked.

"You must think I was attacking you," she said, eyeing the poker.

"I meant the hug."

"I don't need a reason," Madeleine said. "The people I love just know."

Agafon let a gentle smile appear. When she turned back to the hearth, the kindling had burst into flames. She joined Agafon at the table.

When the knocker sounded again, Madeleine stood, anticipating Vladimir. This time, a shorter, younger man appeared. She also led him into the kitchen, where he joined Agafon, and the three of them sat together. When the water in the kettle reached a boil, she dropped in tea leaves and allowed them to steep. After a few minutes, Madeleine picked up the steaming kettle.

"Tea, Agafon, Vladimir?" she asked, holding the kettle in one hand, and a linen towel in the other. The two men invited her to pour it for them.

"Did the landlord see you?" Agafon said. "I know he was making rounds."

"Don't worry," Vladimir insisted. "He shouts louder than he acts."

"You should see what he did to Oleg." Madeleine said.

"What did he do?" Agafon asked.

"Well, he threatened her," Madeleine said.

"He did? With a knife?" Agafon asked.

"With his hands?" Vladimir demanded.

"With his mind," Madeleine clarified, tossing her hair back and wiping her hands on her dress.

"How can a person threaten someone with his mind?" Vladimir insisted, pushing his chair out from the table.

"He has a way of overpowering people," Agafon said, looking at Vladimir. He turned towards Madeleine again, "As he holds something over you."

"That's a good way to put it," Vladimir observed.

"I don't like the way he's doing it. Whatever happened to the Auguliere I knew? You can't trust anyone anymore. Whenever you turn your back, someone's waiting to steal from you. That isn't the Auguliere I remember. I think something evil is going on here."

"Think so?" Agafon wondered.

Vladimir closed his eyes, as though to shut out the discussion. The conversation drifted from topic to topic until they tired. It was quiet as they sipped the last of their tea. Agafon fiddled with fragments of tea leaves, Madeleine stretched out her hands on the table, and Vladimir sat with his arms folded.

The ways of the town settled on their minds like the murk that settles in the bottom of a pond. Madeleine felt the burden of her chores much more than these two able men. She remembered with fondness how her mother had taught her to be dainty. When she reflected on the men, it became apparent to her she did not have to compete with them. Yet, her sick father was no longer the man of the house. These three people continued to let their feelings have center stage as the day advanced.

"Well, I must return to the clerk's office," Vladimir said at last. "Mr. Robertson will be looking for me."

"I need to return to my shop," Agafon said. Madeleine found the strength to show her gratitude to Agafon for the grain with a gracious bow, and she collected the tea cups.

"Thank you, boys," she said as they stood. "It's nice of you to come by my shanty. Thank you for the feed, Agafon. I know I owe you for it."

"I'll get it next time." He smiled and tipped his hat as Vladimir bowed.

"Take care, ma'am." Vladimir said.

"I'll see you at the market," Agafon said. Both men tipped their hats and backed slowly out, leaving Madeleine to reflect on their visit. She decided she needed to leave the house to get fresh air.

Madeleine went out to her coops to find a few more eggs. She took them to the market for three additional rubles. She used one of them to buy bread. She gathered a few tomatoes from her garden. She put these things in a basket and took her pony and cart to the east slope where she purchased preserves. "Why should I give up my hard-earned money to that miser?" Madeleine thought. "He'll just have to wait until I am ready."

When Vladimir returned to his office, Mr. Robertson was already waiting for him, pacing back and forth in front of the door, like an expectant father. Once he saw Vladimir, he stood straight, prepared for a confrontation.

"Long lunch?"

"No, I had some business at Knesnovich's."

"I thought I made it clear we're not running a charity here."

"Yes, but curtailing water use will kill Agafon's corn."

"Don't tell me kindness is an issue here."

"Sir, the failure of the corn supply is detrimental to the cattle feed."

"Are you in love with her, boy?" Vladimir took in a breath.

"Actually, his taxes were contingent upon the Knesnovich's buying his grain."

"Did they?" Mr. Robertson asked. "What are you trying to tell me, that I should extend credit?"

"No, just a little consideration," Vladimir said. "Agafon has to run his shop as well, sir."

"Has he owed taxes as well?"

"Yes, sir."

"Save those thoughts for your emotional entanglements. They have no place in running the village."

"Yes, sir," Vladimir said, looking down at the floor.

In the afternoon, Madeleine drove her pony and cart up the south slope to see her friends Greta Gable and Dana Weiss. They lived high in the meadow. From their house, the whole village lay visible upon the enormous valley floor. Pipes poked out of ceramic roof tiles belching smoke, yielding a burnt wood smell.

She sounded the gray knocker. When Greta opened the door and saw Madeleine, she was so astonished she put her two hands to her cheeks and screamed, "Dana!" gesturing with her hands. "Look who's here!" She took Madeleine into her arms. Dana came to the door. She immediately grabbed Madeleine's hand, and tore her away from Greta.

"I can't believe it," Dana said. Both girls pulled her inside. They stepped back deferentially to examine how beautifully Madeleine had grown up.

"I have a basket for you," Madeleine said.

"Will you look at that!" Greta said.

Madeleine set the basket on the counter of the girls' country home. She noticed everything remained as she remembered it. Heavy drapes hung on the windows, a giant mantel rested over a granite hearth and hot tea always waited in the kettle.

"Why did you do that, Madeleine?" Dana said. "I know your situation." She peeled off the protective flaxen towel. Greta came near and helped empty the basket.

"There's bread, preserves, tomatoes, and fresh eggs."

"Come on in," Greta insisted. She pulled her further into their abode. They seated her on their giant couch, in front of their elaborate hearth.

"Just the other day Greta mentioned something that reminded me of Aunt Emma."

She took out each piece and placed them with care on the counter. Neither girl offered a ruble to Madeleine, however.

"Remember the playhouse?" Madeleine wondered why the girls changed the subject.

"How could I forget?" Madeleine said.

"Is she still alive?" Greta enquired.

"I don't know. Maybe," Dana said.

"We have to visit her one day, Madeleine."

"I heard people say she's dead," Dana said.

"No, she's alive," Madeleine assured them.

"She lives near your sisters, doesn't she?" Greta asked.

"My sisters!" Madeleine said. "Oh, yes. I have sisters."

Greta's words made Madeleine consider the state of her life and her relationship with her two tenebrous sisters, whom she rarely visited since it was too much of a chore. They had all grown up and lived on the other side of the pasture in their father's old house. Even though the sisters maintained the house, they more closely resembled a liability than an asset, as Madeleine remembered them.

"How's your father? Is he . . . ?" Greta cocked her head.

"Same man," Madeleine said. "I can't get him to budge." Madeleine sat on an enormous cushion, letting her dress flare all around her.

"I know what you mean," Dana said. "We had the same thing with Greta's mother. She felt useless once the children grew up."

"Father felt that way about his shop. For years he wouldn't come anywhere near it. It's a drab life." Madeleine creased her lips, letting her dimples show. "I have no life of my own."

"Ever think of leaving?" Dana asked

"Who'll take care of him?" Madeleine wondered, folding her arms defiantly.

"Not the sisters?" Dana strutted past Greta's seat, across from Madeleine. Greta let her carrot-colored hair flop on her back while she and Dana compared glances.

"Yeah!" Madeleine said with an attitude. "The sisters." She sat up straight, crossing her legs. "Everyone wants something."

"Not everyone," Dana said.

"I think as we get older people treat us worse."

"Not all people," Greta said.

"Well, not my two good friends."

"Never!" both girls echoed.

"Besides, the future is full of mysteries," Dana promised.

"Like where will the tax money come from," Greta said. The three girls shared a laugh.

"Wouldn't it be wonderful to go to a mysterious place?" Dana became animated. Greta raised her eyebrows at Dana, while Madeleine watched both girls.

"And meet a mysterious young man!" Greta said, giggling. The two girls focused on Madeleine, who looked back and forth.

"Oh shut up!" Madeleine said, protecting her smile with her hand. All three young women laughed uncontrollably. The deep-seated joy she felt here made her forget about her impending financial burden, at least temporarily.

The kettle rattled, sending its irregular steam whistle out into the room. Greta was quick to fill it with leaves. In moments, she served hot tea. Madeleine sat between the girls, but her mind drifted away from their chatter. She pretended to be with them, laughing and feeling carefree. Deep down, she felt the ominous presence of the landlord invading her mind, not letting her alone. She knew she would have to face him again, before she could rest. The three continued to chat about the happenings in the village, as the sun hid amongst the clouds in the vast valley between two giant mountains.

That same night, after Madeleine returned home, Mr. Robertson came to her shanty. He barged in. Standing tall and lean, looking angry, he lifted his skinny arm and warned, shaking his finger at her, "I told you I must have the tax money or else . . ."

"I got a ruble from my eggs this morning," Madeleine said. "Here."

She picked up the money from the mantel and offered it.

The landlord became amused at the display of plaques and trophies he saw on the mantel.

"Your father was quite a man in his day!"

Madeleine smiled, her bosom swelled with pride as she stood with her hands behind her in the doorway, defending the bedroom. She glanced occasionally over her shoulder at her sleeping father.

"Wouldn't want anything to happen to him," the landlord said.

Madeleine blinked her eyes rapidly. She tried to stand erect and stared at him, but she failed to keep her eyes focused on his face.

"My father helped build Auguliere," she said bravely.

"So he did, child. So he did. His day is gone." He stared directly at her without hesitation. "I will return later in the week for the rest."

Madeleine had known Mr. Robertson since she was a little girl. During that time, she never felt threatened, not like she did now. She really thought he was unfortunate, misguided, and subjugated by his father. She remembered his father's vicious mental assaults on him. She saw the shy young man, who was molded by his robust father, a man of invincible character. His father never failed to reprimand him in public on how to behave. In those days, she never imagined exactly how he could change. He was destined to outgrow his inferiority and emerge as a man consumed with passion. This image still lay vividly in her mind.

As she stood in her kitchen, leaning against the basin, she wondered whether people become cruel naturally as they grew older, or had his father made a tyrant of him? He walked out without speaking, letting her memory fade like her old dress.

Chapter 2

The Cimmerian overcast had cleared. Puffy white clouds scattered, exposing the deep blue sky of the ambrosial valley. Between the giant sloping hills, a young man came to the village outskirts, driving a huge wagon drawn by two colossal horses. On the sides of the wagon placards displayed, "Gilbert & Son, Carpenter and Metallurgist." Most of the townspeople had never seen a horse, with the exception of Madeleine's father and a few other elders.

The young man glimpsed the first settlements in the distance on the edge of the village. He said out loud to himself, "What a lush valley!" One of the horses flapped his lips in the chilly morning air that still clung to the higher slopes. He looked out along the valley floor below him to find himself surrounded by a carpet of green plants. "I think this is tea," he said, scratching his head. "I wonder why there is so much of it?" He pulled the reins again, sending the message to the animals to pull the wagon's load along the road.

The wagon bounced along the dirt road, inching its way to the village, kicking up dust in its wake. When he arrived in the first settlements, several people came out of their shanties to see the display of this noisy contraption. It moved along the dusty, winding road as though it had a mind of its own as it approached the town. When he reached the next settlement, he slowed the wagon down. The driver worked the reins.

"Whoa!" he shouted. "Whoa, there, Larson. Whoa, Nixon!"

Those who gathered on the street were amazed at the way the young man conducted the animals. He pulled the reins back, making the huge beasts rear their heads in the air. The creatures vocalized as they came to a stop. A man staggered to the wagon holding a bottle of spirits. He raised his arm in a threatening gesture. A shopkeeper approached the wagon, still wearing his apron.

"Don't pay any attention to Petrenko. He always makes a scene, especially with newcomers."

"He just enjoys the spirits," the horseman said. "There's no harm in that."

The shopkeeper approached the horseman's wagon, walked all the way around it as if he expected to find something different on the other side. When he was fully satisfied, he stepped up to the wagon's seat and examined the reins and the man who held them.

"Fine animals ya' got there, son."

"They've taken me over the mountains."

"It's been a long time since a horse crossed these parts," the shopkeeper said. "Where you headin'?"

"I was just goin' to pass through until I saw how lush this valley is."

"Lush, sir?" the shopkeeper said. "This is the gloomiest place around and all the crops are dying from the drought. Clouds come every day, yet yield no rain."

"It doesn't seem that way to me," the horseman said. "Look how beautiful the sun is shining." The man stood with his hands outstretched, kicking dirt on his shadow on the ground.

"Why do you like our valley?" the shopkeeper asked.

The horseman didn't answer right away. He reflected on it, pointing his chin up, scratching his clean-shaven face and letting it feel the full rays of the sun.

"I love the way the blue sky came out early in the mornin'." The shopkeeper looked up at the horseman as he climbed down.

"We haven't seen the blue sky here in weeks, sir," the shopkeeper said. The young man stretched and took in a breath. The shopkeeper folded his arms.

"Weeks, is it?" One of the horses shook his head, fluttering his lips.

"Most of the time it's dismal," the shopkeeper said. "It might shine for a mornin', but not again for a while. Why would anyone want to come here?" He noticed the horseman's shadow in the bright sun.

"Look how green your meadows are."

"Aye, they are . . ."

"I felt a wee bit of a callin'," the horseman said.

"A callin'?" The curious shopkeeper said, tilting his head.

"A wee bit, sir," the horseman insisted. Then the other horse shook his head. "This valley suits me just fine. My name is Gilbert, like it says on the sign." Gilbert pointed back to the wagon's side.

"They call me Agafon." They shook hands. Agafon looked over the wagon carefully, pulling on his scruffy red beard. When he was satisfied, he said, "Does our village seem to be in need?"

"Not at all, sir. I can feel the life of this place dwindling. I am the one who can rejuvenate it with my skills."

"We do need skilled souls here. There's been a presence here holding folks back."

"I think the place needs me."

"Well now," Agafon said, scratching his beard, "maybe it does." Agafon stepped back again, "You can find stores that sell survival goods down the road. I have a shop here for heavy equipment, should the need arise. The blacksmith is on the east edge." Agafon indicated his shop with a head gesture. Gilbert nodded, climbing back up on the seat of his wagon. Agafon spun around and returned to his shop, saying on the way, "We'll meet again. I'll always be here," letting his voice echo from the buildings on the street." Gilbert waved his hand and grabbed the reins.

"Yaw!" and the horses started to pull the massive wagon.

As the giant vehicle rolled along the dusty road, Gilbert listened to a metallic clinking sound in the distance. It didn't sound like bells exactly. It sounded a lot more like odd pieces of metal making contact with each other through random movement. Their pitch varied and the sound grew louder as the wagon bumped along. Then the source of the sound appeared. A herd of cattle crossed the road like angry men walking in a squatting position. The cattle blocked Gilbert's wagon once they fully entered the road. He observed gray bells attached around their necks, making a low-pitched clinking sound as they moved. Their hooves also clanked, but made a different sound, more of a blunt sound, on the cobblestones. The shepherd who drove them waved, indicating the end of their run. Gilbert was at last able to resume, more amused than before.

In the center of town, past the big well, he noticed tall and skinny trees crowded together in one of the parks. He listened to the loud noise of crickets among the trees. On a side street, opposite the park, a shop stood with a large window display. Gilbert noticed the building was made of solid brick. A red light glowed from inside. Outside, a sign read, "Mrs. Teivel, Reader & Advisor." When he halted the wagon, he climbed down from the rig with care, collecting the reins to tie them to the hitching post on the street. He stepped up, onto the high boards of the walkway. Here, he got a good look at the shop window. Opposite, a large sign read *County Clerk's Office*. He looked alternately at the two places, wondering why they were opposite. He made some questionable discoveries in Auguliere, which made him feel something inconsistent was going on that he didn't understand.

Mrs. Teivel's shop was dark and dingy. It looked like nothing he had ever seen before. In Mrs. Teivel's shop, an old, short woman sat in a tattered dress by the window amidst the shadows of the shop. She kept her head down, squeezing her chin into her chest. Curiosity motivated Gilbert to enter the shop. She turned to face him squarely, unflinching, looking below his eyes, from behind a protective counter. Gilbert retained a surprised expression. She spoke without hesitation in a natural flow that suited her.

"I know the face of the stranger here from over the hills and in another land. He comes to seek his fortune and reeks of bad command."

"I am just visiting," Gilbert said. "Maybe I can find work here." The old woman looked up, twitching one eye, letting the other eye wander while she bobbed her head in a peculiar way.

"Trouble, trouble, moil and rubble . . . Misery wish or curse your double."

"I do not wish to make trouble, madam."

"Silence him whose face bears stubble, all things reduced again to rubble."

"I don't understand."

"Then you need to dismiss this rubble and slowly let him know."

"Know?" Gilbert asked. "Know what?"

"Use your wit, use your hand . . . take the devil's contraband."

This woman made his skin itch, causing incessant scratching. Gilbert stood limply against the high counter. The old woman reminded him of a scolding school teacher. She remained standing, blinking the good eye, while all the time making motions of hand-washing. Gilbert could not tell whether she gestured for money or merely exhibited strange habits. He was ready to pay her, but she made no verbal demand for it. Still baffled, he sensed a surge of adrenalin as he backed up to the door. Feeling no resistance, he backed out of the store carefully, tipping his wide-brimmed hat as he exited, thanking the woman for her time. As he turned around in the broad daylight, a young man stood on the street, ready to greet him. Mud had caked on his boots. Gilbert's candid exchange with the young man returned him to a normal state of mind.

"She's a mindful." The young man smiled, stroked his smooth, black beard, and admired his dog. The canine greeted him with a whimper, dropped his head, and let his tongue thrash about.

"Wonder why her shop's made of red stone?" queried Gilbert.

"Her shop's the only structure in Auguliere that is made of red stone."

"Yeah?"

"The rest are made of wood."

"I wonder why?" Gilbert said. The man just shrugged his shoulders in response.

"I'm Vladimir and this here's Chipper." Chipper's feet were also muddy. The animal first looked back at Vladimir as if to ask permission to lick Gilbert's fingers. Gilbert placed a hand on the dog to pet him instinctively while he looked straight into Vladimir's eyes.

"What a beautiful coat!" Gilbert said. "And such a golden color. He's really nice." Gilbert looked down at the animal. "Good boy," he said, feeling completely at home around animals.

"I saw your cart," Vladimir said. "I've never seen ponies so large before. Are they from another land?" Gilbert laughed, surprising Vladimir.

"They are indeed from another land," Gilbert said. "We call them horses!"

"Horses," Vladimir said more seriously. "What a quaint name."

"They're wonderful animals."

"So where are you parking them for the night?"

"I was looking for a stable."

"There's one at old Iakov Knesnovich's abandoned shop on Sycamore Lane.

"Will he mind?"

"Hasn't used the place in years. He'd be happy to rent it out."

"Thanks much, my friend."

"Just drive your horses up the road past two large wooden buildings, past the big well, and turn right. You'll see another large wooden structure with a wide door on the front with a dirt floor inside," Vladimir said. Gilbert tipped his hat. "Anything you need, just ask. I am the county clerk."

The two young men took each other's arms tightly, then parted. Chipper followed Vladimir, occasionally looking back at Gilbert's wagon. As he rode away, he noticed something very strange. People standing and walking in the streets gawked at the wagon in an odd way. Gilbert sensed people's thoughts. He perceived fear in people, but it was unclear to him what they were afraid of. This puzzled him because he could not see anything to fear. He drove the wagon slowly, keeping himself attuned to the strangers passing as he rode. He was beginning to realize it was the feeling of concern that made him aware of his needed presence in Auguliere.

Two wide doors concealed the stable on Sycamore Lane. Gilbert climbed down from the wagon and pulled open the heavy doors. He peered into the darkness. No one occupied the place, inside or out. At first the animals hesitated, but Gilbert quieted them by talking softly to them as though they were children.

"Take it easy, Larson." He stroked the horse's mane, and then turned to the other one. "Nixon, old boy," he said.

"Take it easy, fellow. Easy!"

He held the beast's head firmly with both hands, reassuring him with a date. When they calmed down, he drove them into the darkness inside. Gilbert unhitched them and removed their bridles, and led them to a hitching post inside. Each one shook his head in silence, but remained still.

Gilbert climbed into the wagon. Containers filled with supplies lined the sides of the interior. Among the supplies, several layers of blankets made a comfortable bed. Sitting on the bed, he pulled off his boots, catching a whiff of foot odor, and snuggled under the covers. Through the canopy's opening he stared at the uneven boards on the stable's gigantic rafters. The window on the side of the stable gave a view of a shanty's window. He only saw the flicker of candlelight through it. He fell quickly into slumber, exhausted from his arduous journey. He awoke occasionally to see the stars through cracks in the ceiling and the moonlight crept in behind the shadow of the door, in the eerie stillness. He could not understand people's apprehension since he thought Auguliere appeared to be such a peaceful place to settle.

Chapter 3

The next morning the horses' whinnies awoke Gilbert. When he crawled out of the front of the wagon, his eyes met the loveliest young woman he had ever seen. Her somber expression blossomed into a broad smile with a dimple that formed in one cheek. Gilbert sat on the edge of the wagon's seat, and tried to appear awake. Rays of light had just started to filter through the cracks in the roof of the old stable, landing on the stark dirt floor. Birds sat on the shingle's ragged edges, casting their silhouettes in the bright areas, and sang to welcome the morning sun.

"My father owns this stable," the young woman said, stepping closer and brushing her dress with her hands. Gilbert gulped. "You can keep your animals here. I see you're a carpenter." Her eyes probed his sleepy face. Gilbert shook his head in affirmation. She pinched her lips together as though she knew his motivation.

"Yes," Gilbert said, more alert, "as the sign says." He looked over his shoulder at the wagon's side. "I am a carpenter and metallurgist. I can build tools with wood and metal."

Gilbert, looking around, pushed himself up until he slid off the seat, landing in front of her.

"Are there any bricks about?" Gilbert asked. "Can I buy mortar?"

"Bricks are hard to come by," Madeleine said. "There are shops around that have mortar, but they haven't been very busy lately." Now she let dimples form on both cheeks. She stood limp against a post, letting one knee bend. The brown hair floated gently over her shoulders. Her dress flared as she turned.

"This building is awfully drafty and the roof leaks. I saw the stars through it last night." Gilbert glided the back of his hand over the stubble of his clean-shaven face, stepping back.

"I'm sorry if it was uncomfortable," Madeleine said, looking at him oddly.

"It wasn't. I just thought I could repair it." He looked up at the cracks, watching the birds thoughtfully.

"You're different," observed Madeleine.

"I'm still a man," the young carpenter said.

"I can see that indeed you are!" She shifted to maintain her dignity. "You are strange, Mr. Gilbert," she said. "Nobody does deeds around here anymore."

"It's Gilbert O'Sullivan, ma'am," Gilbert said. "I would be happy to."

"You're not from around here, are you?"

"No, ma'am."

"That would be nice, Mr. O'Sullivan." She extended her delicate hand, blinking her eyes shyly. "I'm Madeleine." He took her hand gently, peeking at her soft skin. He looked down and smiled.

"Please call me Gilbert," the carpenter insisted. "Whenever something needs fixin', you can always count on me."

"You say that now, but when the time really comes, you'll find excuses like most people do."

"Let it be known that I am a man of my word. You may test my integrity!" Gilbert stepped away from the wagon. He stood so much taller that he still looked down on her.

"Maybe I will." Gilbert stimulated Madeleine's memories of her father. She could still smell the pine resin in the glue basins and the fresh smell of the cut maple and white birch. She regarded the floor near her feet, upon which she vividly remembered playing. Gilbert examined the same area, but only found the naked floor.

"I couldn't help notice the endless rows of aspen trees in the parks."

"Nobody uses them," Madeleine said, still looking down.

"The trees?"

"The parks. I never really noticed the trees."

"How could you not notice them?" Gilbert said. Madeleine blushed. Only her mother had the power to do that, according to her father. It seemed so long ago she forgot. Now, the blush caught her off guard, leaving her feeling embarrassed. Somehow, Gilbert continued to stimulate her memories.

"Maybe I can take one or two of them down."

Madeleine shrugged her shoulders. "What will you do with them?" she asked, looking up at him.

"Use the wood."

"Nobody will mind." Madeleine turned around, trying to hide her blush, and studied the wagon. "My father was a carpenter, too." Gilbert stepped back near his horse.

"Oh, yeah?" he said with interest.

"He built most of the village. Everywhere you look you will find the work of his hand." Madeleine moved closer.

"You must be proud." Gilbert petted his horse. The animal raised his head, and let it bob.

"My father used to say, 'A man with good hands needs to use tools to fabricate things.'"

"It's a wise saying."

"My father is a wise man," Madeleine assured him. "There's a shop in the corner and a bed inside. I'm afraid there's not much light. Father never had the chance to build a skylight."

"I shall build it, and I have oil for a lamp and polished metal reflectors to increase the illumination. This will allow me to work at night, increasing my productivity. You will see."

"I can't believe you will do all that." Madeleine couldn't help think of her father again. She couldn't remember that he ever used polished metal reflectors.

"I will keep my word," Gilbert promised. She saw an unusual honesty in him, which she never knew from the villagers. She was astonished to see it in a stranger.

"Time will dictate if you do." She lifted her chin aristocratically.

"I understand trust must be earned," Gilbert confirmed. "I will show you."

"You are resourceful," Madeleine observed. "I will check on your progress."

"I am in your debt," Gilbert said.

"No," Madeleine snapped, letting her blush return, "you should never be in anyone's debt!" Tears then filled her eyes. She pulled herself back, wiping her cheeks with her sleeve. Gilbert withdrew from her, surprised to see such an emotional outburst. Somehow, Madeleine felt responsible for his concern, but she remained quiet.

"Did I say something wrong?" Gilbert wondered, scratching his already irritated head.

"No," Madeleine assured, trying to control her weeping."Just something I was thinking about." She turned to approach the big door of the rickety stable.

"Might I pay you two rubles for the place?" Gilbert called.

Madeleine turned again, facing Gilbert.

"You are kind," she said, pushing her hair back and shaking her head.

"It is only fitting I pay rent for the use of your father's shop and stable. After all, I am using it to keep my horses, do my work and as an inn. Would two rubles per week be fair?"

"It is more than fair. Thank you. You are generous." Madeleine composed herself. Gilbert climbed back up on the wagon. He rummaged through his belongings until he found a small burlap sack. He reached into it and pulled out two coins.

"Here," he said, reaching out to Madeleine. She took the currency graciously. She turned and happily advanced to the street.

"I will give you a chance," she said, waving her hand as she walked off. "I will keep my word."

She left him to explore the edifice. When he found the shop, he was drawn to it. He saw that it contained an ancient worktable, adorned with a vise at one end and an anvil at the other. He paused, reflecting on the power that he realized these objects possessed and what he could accomplish with them. A hearth filled the opposite wall. He stood midway between the hearth and worktable and whispered: "Why is that girl so troubled in such a perfect place?"

CHAPTER 4

Later in the afternoon, Mr. Robertson entered Mrs. Teivel's shop. She immediately stood amidst a clutter of ornaments and approached the high counter. Mr. Robertson removed his top hat and bowed his narrow head, allowing the stringy combed-back hair to fall to the side. His skinny face invaded her mysterious space with trepidation.

"I learned a newcomer has arrived here. Have you made his acquaintance?" he said, brushing back a long black strand. She stared at his straggly beard, squinting her good eye. The chubby arms lay folded over the counter.

"From over the hills, from another land . . . a stranger comes with bad command."

"And what seeks he?" The landlord stared deep into the woman's unusual eyes.

"He seeks no vice . . . owes no tax. The wood he'll splice be from his ax." The woman sat, tightening her folded arms. "Her heart will thump, your cat will purr. You need give me five rubles, sir." He gaped at the woman, amazed by her commands. The landlord reached into the slovenly suit pocket and pulled out money. He counted it out carefully, then he put it down on the counter, making a grimace. She picked up the currency slowly and counted it just as carefully. The two people looked at each other with some degree of satisfaction. Then he walked out of the shop.

While he was in town, he visited Madeleine. This time, she was ready for him. Whenever the landlord came around, the neighbors' dogs would start barking. It was her warning signal. She had the chance to mentally prepare to confront him. He opened the door as though it were his. Madeleine stood at the threshold directly in front of his leering presence. She examined him, paying careful attention to his facial expressions.

"You are early."

"I'm in town," the landlord said, displaying an artificial smile. "Have you the money?" Madeleine withdrew from his countenance and sat down at her kitchen table. The landlord followed her into the house, but he remained standing.

"I can pay the two rubles I owe from last month."

"And this month?"

"I have a new source." She sat with her elbows on the table, letting her palms support her chin. She looked up at the callous face with a simple smile.

"What is the nature of this source?" the landlord said, shifting his weight from one foot to the other. Madeleine folded her arms proudly.

"I found a tenant for my father's shop."

"How touching, child."

"He is a good man."

"Is he worth rent?"

She stood, approached the mantel, took two coins from a box, and handed the rubles to him. He counted them several times during which he observed the unusual smile she allowed to appear, as though she were mocking him. She tried to squint her eyes shyly in the dim light.

"I know you want more," she said. "Return next week." He suddenly reached out, grabbed her tender arm, and delivered a penetrating stare into her gentle brown eyes. When she tried to struggle free of his grip, he held her tighter, preventing her escape. She stood up to him so they were face-to-face. He stared at her staunchly.

"My patience is wearing thin, girl." He let go of her, causing her to stumble. He turned toward the door, sneering again before he departed. Madeleine had thought he'd never leave. She pulled back her sleeve to expose the red mark the landlord inflicted on her arm. She rubbed the spot softly, remembering the pain and humiliation she experienced. She stretched around to look at the spot again, feeling violated.

"Is everything okay, dear?" her father babbled from his sick bed, with a gurgling voice, coughing a few times. He cleared his throat before Madeleine answered.

"It is now, father. Tomorrow I shall visit the carpenter." He coughed again.

"Why don't you bring this young man here so I can meet him?"

"Father!" Madeleine said.

"Madeleine," her father pleaded. "Just let me see who's occupying my shop."

She picked up her big basket from the table, regarded its emptiness and felt ashamed. She knew the landlord would be back, more determined than ever. She also realized she could share this pain with no one, not even the carpenter.

CHAPTER 5

The next afternoon Madeleine contemplated visiting the stable, but she felt ashamed to bother the new tenant so quickly. She let a week pass before the urge to visit resurfaced. When she entered, she found Gilbert working. She almost didn't recognize the place. As she moved inside, she was immersed in Gilbert's workshop. Partially finished items hung from the rafters, and several tables displayed ongoing projects. Buckets of glue from pine resin littered the floor just the way she remembered them from her father, and everywhere planks of fresh aspen stood against the walls.

"You are industrious," she said. "Where did you get all this?"

"I took them from the aspen trees in the park. Each gave me several planks." She saw a table with an unusual tool rising from an opening in it.

"What is this contraption?" she pointed.

"Oh, do you think it will make too much noise?"

"I wasn't even thinking about that," Madeleine said, rubbing her eyes. Dust had risen in the air, reminding her of another time in her life. "Just wondering what it was."

"We call it a saw mill."

"How does it work?" She flung her hair to one side and looked at the machinery more eagerly.

"A pedal rotates back and forth, pushing a lever around the wheel. This turns the shaft which turns the blade." He pointed.

"The saw blade is made into a circle. How can you saw wood that way?" Gilbert laughed. He took her by the hand, leading her to a bench. He beckoned her to sit while he returned to the machine to demonstrate it.

"Watch and I will show you." She observed the operation with interest. He placed one of the planks lengthwise on the table. He started the machine. Slowly he fed the plank into the turning blade. Madeleine was fascinated by the way the blade chewed through the wood effortlessly.

"It's loud, but amazing," she said. "How did you figure that out?"

"I didn't. My father taught me."

"Oh, yes. That's why it says Gilbert & Son on your wagon?"

"Yes, it is."

"Where is your father?"

"He is in the ground." Madeleine bowed her head in sorrow. It made her consider her own father's mortality. "He's in a good place now," Gilbert said. "He suffered a vile disease for many years." Madeleine could feel the pain emanating from Gilbert's glistening eyes. She pressed her fingers to her moistened lips and cringed.

"I'm sorry," she said, feeling incredibly helpless.

"Don't feel sorry," Gilbert said with pride. "He taught me everything he knew. He was a wonderful man." Madeleine mentally compared her father with his.

"That's how I feel about my father."

"He is still with you?"

"He is, but he's sick. I don't know how long he can hang on. He will be real happy to meet you." Madeleine smiled provocatively. Gilbert began milling the planks into long boards as Madeleine watched. He cut the boards to length and trimmed the edges with his ax. It was obvious he was skilled. In fact, he knew how to drill holes in the boards with a brace to insert wooden pegs that fastened pieces together. He had built carts, toys, and tools. When the grain of the wood made a bend, he knew to carve around the bend to make Johnson bars. Gilbert knew how to make mallets, templates for plaster of Paris molds and handles for chisels and hammers. He let nothing go to waste, using the bark to make strands, which he wove into baskets. The carpenter had hauled hemp from the meadows and separated the stringy fibers into strands that he braided together to make rope.

The sight of all of Gilbert's work brought Madeleine back to earlier times. She had visions of running into this shop with her father calling her. She also remembered her mother calling, *"Madeleine, your supper's getting cold. You two must come home at once!"*

Gilbert placed the pieces he had fashioned on a shelf he had built in a corner of the shop, along with the other finished work. Contentment filled his consciousness. Madeleine admired Gilbert's craftsmanship. A feeling of well being came over her as she watched him work. "You must be hungry," she said, inhaling deeply. She recalled how her mother catered to her husband as he worked. "I'm going back to my shanty to make lunch for you."

"You know, you certainly don't have to do all that . . ."

"You're right, Gilbert. I don't have to do it. *I want to do it.*" She smiled with intensified determination. She scampered away as Gilbert continued his work. In a few minutes, Madeleine returned to the stable with a frayed basket full of fresh rolls, fruit picked from the meadows and cooked grains. Gilbert smiled and ate the food slowly, glancing at Madeleine shyly, appreciating Madeleine's domestic efforts. Madeleine watched Gilbert devour the food, keeping the feeling of satisfaction to herself.

As he sat on the edge of his wagon, Larson swung his head around to acknowledge the carpenter's presence. Nixon gently nuzzled his shoulder until the animal forced Gilbert to affirm his proximity. He sat motionless for a moment, letting his brow relax and permitting his tired face to show how hard he had worked. Madeleine observed his joyful feeling of accomplishments from the day's work.

"My animals have done the really hard work. I must find a meal for them."

"Agafon's shop has grains," Madeleine said. "You can get oats there." Madeleine knew Gilbert had found his place and was ready to carry out his life's mission. What she didn't know was how it would affect her. "I know I've been a pest, disturbing your tranquility."

"No, you haven't. Your company is always refreshing. And dinner! I will show my gratitude. Wait and see."

Madeleine continued to reminisce and smiled as she watched him consume the last of his dinner.

CHAPTER 6

Two more weeks passed. Madeleine didn't want Gilbert to consider her a pest by watching him work every day. She was able to see him come and go through the window. Finally, the urgency of her curiosity reached a level she couldn't tolerate anymore, compelling her to visit Gilbert's shop. He was working in the shop when Madeleine came.

"Mornin'," Madeleine said, pushing open the huge door.

"Mornin', ma'am," Gilbert said. He tipped his soiled hat. "What a wonderful village it is."

"It is," Madeleine said. "Were you able to find grain for your animals?"

"Agafon is a wonderful man. He gave me all I needed. He also showed me some great trails on the slopes."

"Be careful on the slopes," Madeleine said. "Dangers lurk there."

"Here are the four rubles I owe you for the next rent."

"Oh, I am sorry," Madeleine admitted. "I did not pass here to collect the rent. I wanted to see what you are building."

"They say that it's always gloomy here. They say that the sky is always overcast."

"That's what they say."

"That is not true. The sun has been shining every day for the last two weeks. Ever since I got here I noticed the warmth of this place. Can that be a coincidence? Everything seems to fall into place. If it is, I remain impressed by your incredible valley."

"Maybe you brought it with you." She fluttered her eyelids. Gilbert acknowledged her with a smile.

He stepped closer, holding on to a piece of lumber. "I want to show you something." He set the wood down on the workbench, took her hand and led her to the outer wall of the shop. All Gilbert's finished work amazed her. A giant rack of items stood against the wall. Madeleine couldn't believe it. Gilbert reached for a basket and some rope. "Please take them. I know you need implements and I have so many."

"I never met anyone so kind. People here are not always so kind. People tell you one thing and they do the opposite behind your back. You can't trust anyone. Everyone's afraid of the landlord. You see, he owns most of the land, collects rent. What he doesn't own, he collects taxes on. Either way, he's a miser."

"Don't worry about him. We will take care of ourselves."

"What will you do with all these things?"

"There's more," he led her again, to another part of the structure where he had built a room. Inside, she saw things that reminded her of her childhood.

"I haven't seen anything like this in years."

"Like it?" There were stacks of handmade toys on every shelf.

"Where did you get them?"

"I made them." Madeleine found it hard to believe. Once she examined them, it was clear to her Gilbert hand made all the toys.

"My father used to make these," Madeleine examined a toy.

"The aspen wood is so wonderful with which to work."

"Funny no one ever noticed the trees before."

"Where did your father get his wood?"

"We used to get shipments of wood from far away places. Wagons pulled by mules used to bring them into the valley."

"Can you take these toys to the children?"

"Of course I can."

"I can see how much this town needs a carpenter. I built crates for old man Billings, put new rails on Winthrop's coops, and Sanders needed his fence mended. I've been busy." Madeleine reflected for a moment.

"Yes," she said. "I guess this town does need a carpenter. Can I take those toys now?" Madeleine asked.

"They are all on the shelf. I will get them."

"My father wanted to . . . will you come to our house?" Madeleine finally blurted. Gilbert looked at her, unsure of how to react until Madeleine smiled to let him know he would feel invited. Gilbert displayed his own smile.

"I would love to," Gilbert said.

"Tomorrow?" Madeleine said. "At the end of your workday."

"Thank you, Madeleine," Gilbert said. "I will be there as you mentioned."

"I have my wagon and pony," Madeleine said. "It would be my pleasure to help you with the toys."

Madeleine went out of the stable to hitch up her pony. She brought her wagon around to the stable, and pulled her pony into the barn. Gilbert helped her load up the toys. He was careful to arrange them so they would not get damaged on their way. Madeleine drove her pony to the market square. The gray cowbells made a clanking noise from the vibration of the cobblestones, attracting attention. When she halted the wagon, she lifted one of the toys. The wooden toy drew the children's attention. She moved the parts, further stimulating the children's interest. One child approached. He looked up at Madeleine in the wagon and said, "Can I have one?" Madeleine smiled and offered it to the child. "Oh, thank you, thank you." The child was happier than anyone could remember. His mother came up to Madeleine.

"Where did you get these toys, young lady?"

"Why, from the carpenter, ma'am."

"The carpenter?" the woman said, examining the toy. "Who is this carpenter? When did he arrive in Auguliere?"

"He's a gentle man who came from over the hills a few days ago," Madeleine said. Other women took interest in the discussion.

"The carpenter?"

"What carpenter?" said another woman.

"I didn't know we had a carpenter," another woman called.

"Let me offer you a ruble for this trinket," the first mother said. The woman reached into her bag and pulled out her purse. She found a coin and offered it.

"Thank you, ma'am," she said. Others approached the wagon.

"Give me the chest," one woman said.

"I want the doll," a little girl yelled.

"I see a train," a boy called. "Can I get it, mother?"

"Sure, son," the mother said. "Here's a ruble, young lady." She handed over the coin. Madeleine slipped it into her pocket.

Madeleine was deluged with requests. Each time a woman offered money, a child walked away with a toy. When the flurry of people subsided, Madeleine found herself sitting in an empty wagon with a pocket of her dress filled with coins.

One small child ambled up to the wagon, looked up and said, "Can I get a toy?"

"I'm sorry, son," she said, "I don't have any more." The child began to cry, making Madeleine feel sorry.

"I will bring more tomorrow." She reached out to pat the boy on his head. "Now go back to your mother and tell her what I said."

"Yes, miss," he said and ran off to his mother.

Madeleine sat alone for a long moment with her hands inside her pocket, flicking the coins back and forth. She finally pulled the coins out, dumping them onto the wagon bed. She instinctively counted them one by one until she got to the last two, counting, "Forty-nine . . . fifty!" she turned to see the last few people leaving the square. She tilted her head in disbelief. She looked up into the sky. "Fifty!" she shouted. She looked down at the pile of coins and began to cry.

Chapter 7

The cool mountain breeze had pushed open the big door of Gilbert's shop. A boy wandered into it. He sat on a chunk of wood and didn't move or speak. He looked at all the activity in the shop until Gilbert noticed him. Once Gilbert approached him, the boy stood up with a scared expression. The big man moved over closer to him wearing a tremendous smile. The boy remained frozen with fear. Even when Gilbert spoke gently to the boy, he held back.

"Hey, son," he said, maintaining his smile. "How'd you like to see my shop?"

The boy stared straight ahead for a long while, motionless. Gilbert tried to take his hand to lead him into the shop, but the boy was reluctant, pulled back his hand, and stood stiffly. Gilbert was baffled. Then he said, "Wait here, son." He advanced to the little room near his shop and disappeared inside briefly. When he emerged, the boy struggled to see what he carried; Gilbert brought the object closer to the boy. His eyes opened wide. He examined the toy and looked at Gilbert. The boy regarded the object apprehensively, but kept staring at it until Gilbert finally offered it to him. He hesitated at first to take it. Gilbert gradually encouraged him by demonstrating its movements. A smile lit up his face as he took it and began to play with it.

"Can you say 'thank you'?" Gilbert asked. The boy did not answer.

After a while, Gilbert had a chance to examine him carefully. He noticed the child had a cleft palate. Gilbert immediately showed understanding, and didn't ask the boy to speak again. Instead, he continued to play with the boy. Gilbert kept a smile on his face all the time they played. Gilbert took him by the hand and led him into the shop where he showed him all the tools. The tools in the shop intrigued him. He wanted to touch everything, even the circular saw blade. Gilbert gently warned him about the dangers of touching it by showing him how sharp the teeth were. The boy nodded, indicating he understood the perils in the shop, showing respect for Gilbert.

After an hour, a frail woman approached the big door. She heard nothing, but hesitated to step inside. She struggled to see into the dark shadows. Finally, she saw the shadow of her son against the strong ray of sunlight through the door. When the door squeaked, Gilbert turned around and came into view. He saw the woman's dark silhouette against the sunlight, as she stood nervously next to the door. Gilbert brought out the smiling boy promptly like a proud big brother. She was surprised to see his joyful expression. She seldom saw him happy and was suspicious of Gilbert.

"Where were you?" she asked. "You know not to wander into strange places."

"He's a fine boy, ma'am," Gilbert said, coming closer. "Can I know his name?" The woman only stared at Gilbert, making him feel uncomfortable.

"Come along, Pavel," she said. Gilbert smiled at the woman. She returned a cold stare. The boy smiled again broadly and pointed to Gilbert with one hand, holding the toy with the other.

"Now give the man back his property." The boy declined and withdrew. Gilbert spoke up in his defense.

"It's a gift, ma'am," Gilbert said. "A boy needs a toy."

The woman pulled the lad away, admonishing him in whispers, looking over her shoulder as they walked along. Gilbert leaned against his lumber stack, wondering how the boy's mother would reprimand him. He somehow felt responsible.

Chapter 8

Gilbert sounded the gray knocker. In a few seconds, he heard scuffling behind the door. In another moment, it opened, and Madeleine stood on the threshold as radiant as ever. Gilbert took a deep breath. Madeleine saw that he was nervous and fidgety. She extended her soft hand and led him in.

"Ev'nin', ma'am!" Gilbert said, tipping his ragged hat. She bowed gracefully, stepping back to let him enter the modest domicile. She saw the doorway barely accommodated him as he dipped his head instinctively. She led him into the common kitchen.

"Please sit at our humble table," Madeleine said. "I am sorry our home is so small. It only has three rooms and father occupies one of them. The other is mine. We can bake bread here and roast meat."

"It is kind of you to invite me to share your table."

"Grain soup with wild mushrooms picked at the edge of the meadow near the pines is ready. We have homemade bread."

Madeleine said nothing as she prepared the place settings. She ladled the soup into a bowl and placed it before Gilbert. Gilbert licked his lips, taking in the bounty of food before him.

"It's all from the land. They're not all my father's grains," Madeleine said. "Some come from the neighbors' property. I give them my eggs in exchange. I don't sell all the eggs. We share many things here in Auguliere."

Madeleine's father heard their talking. He rose from his bed and maneuvered himself into his wheel chair. He wheeled himself into the kitchen.

"This is the gentleman?" he said.

"Yes, father." Madeleine reflected on times past.

"I'm Iakov Knesnovich," her father said, eager to join them at the table. "Social occasions are rare in the Knesnovich house."

"Gilbert O'Sullivan." Gilbert pinched his lips together tightly, gesturing approval.

Her father adjusted his chair at the table, and extended his hand. Gilbert partially rose to accept Iakov's hand.

"Your daughter was just telling me how she trades eggs and grain to prepare such a wonderful meal. It seems to me people in this place are very communal," Gilbert noted.

"Yes, they are," Iakov said.

"Then why is everyone so sad?" Gilbert inquired, as he settled back in his chair.

"We used to have a giant pine tree brought down from the alpine meadows each year," Iakov said, dribbling the soup on his shirt.

"Oh father," Madeleine said. "Look at you!"

"Show him the artist sketch, child," he managed to say while she fussed with him.

"Leave it be, father." Madeleine motioned back to the sketch's location to discourage showing it. Gilbert glanced at it, hanging over the mantel.

"We used to erect it in the square, in the middle of the market to celebrate Christmas," Madeleine said. "We decorated it with ornaments the women made. An elderly man, who made toys, used to give them to the children at Christmas time. He made toys out of wood, just like you do. We used to have giant maple trees along the streets in the village. They started to die because they were old. So, men cut them and used their wonderful white wood to fabricate many needed things, much like you have done." The discussion was mesmerizing Gilbert, but Iakov was yawning.

"So what happened to them?" Gilbert said.

"The landlord disapproved," Madeleine said. "After mother died, everything changed."

"He passed an ordinance," Iakov said in a sheepish tone.

"That's when people became afraid of him," Madeleine said. "He is heartless, especially to the children."

She looked to her father for agreement, but his eyes were rolling and he became less aware of dinner.

"Then why don't people just leave and go to another village?" Gilbert suggested.

"Everyone was born here. Auguliere is all they know. It is not in them to move," Madeleine said. She stood and pulled her father's chair away from the table, daubing his chin with a flaxen towel. "Besides, my father needs me."

"Yes, that is true," Iakov said, nodding in agreement. "Some day this town will modernize. You will see people from all over the world, even from the New World."

"The New World," Madeleine said. "Now really, father."

"Mark my word! People will come to visit, just to see the majesty of our magnificent green valley with an endless tea plantation. I know it will come to pass. Maybe your grandchildren will get to see it."

Madeleine reflected on the essence of her home life and family, fondly remembering her sisters' petty conflicts. Her mother had earned a special niche in her heart. She could not imagine doing anything without first thinking of how her mother would act.

Madeleine thought her mother had been the most resourceful woman she ever knew. It made Madeleine become the nurturing woman she was. Her father needed that. To him, it was almost like a gift from his deceased wife, through their daughter. Madeleine always gave him the same comfort, as if it came directly from his wife.

Her mother would also cast shadows of doubt on everything. Once she died, Madeleine was convinced her mother had been right; that no one could ever be fully trusted. These thoughts rambled in Madeleine's mind, and made her apprehensive.

"Others need you, too," Gilbert suggested.

"Perhaps," Madeleine admitted, watching her father nodding off again. "My roots are here." She regarded him with her head cocked to one side.

"I saw something different about you," Gilbert said, observing her lowering her head. "Your face tells another story."

Iakov slept soundly. His head drooped to one side. Madeleine stood and found a pillow to cushion his head. He reacted a little to her repositioning his head, but stayed asleep as Madeleine wheeled him back to his room.

"Since I was a child," Madeleine continued, returning to the kitchen, "I wanted to know what lies beyond the mountain pass, but we are scared. Wild animals have been seen there, and they have been known to eat people."

"Really?"

"Yes, really. There are stories."

"I came through that pass and they didn't eat me." Madeleine pushed her lips together while glancing up at Gilbert.

"That's because you are a strong man," she said, playing with her spoon in the soup.

"Does that make me invincible?"

"Besides, you have the protection of your big wagon and your two enormous horses."

"They are large animals," Gilbert admitted.

"You are an explorer," Madeleine said. "We are simple country folks."

"Fear not the unknown," Gilbert insisted. "Learn from its mysteries."

"From childhood we are taught by everyone to be afraid."

"Then we shall overcome this fear together." Madeleine could only smile.

"It's easy to say what you ought to do. Acting on it is another matter."

"I quite agree with you. However, persistence is indelible in a person's character. If you really want to succeed, you must forge ahead. You can only know victory once you've experienced defeat."

"My father is defeated," Madeleine said, motioning back to the room. "Look at him."

"He looks peaceful to me."

"You mean try to get something even though you know you can't get it?"

"Not exactly," Gilbert said. "You need to set realistic goals."

"What would be a realistic goal?"

"If you look out to the North Slope, you will see some gray rock. One day I want to explore it with the hope of discovering ore."

"What is ore?" Madeleine quizzed him.

"It is the rock from which my father taught me to smelt metal." Gilbert continued to eat. "This is delicious."

"What would you do with this metal?" She fluffed her brown hair impatiently.

"I have noticed all the door knockers and all the cow bells are made from the same gray metal."

"What is it?"

"We call it zinc."

"I never knew what it was. My father had only mentioned it briefly."

"I'll bet your father realizes its value."

"So, you can make knockers and bells?"

"It has a much greater use than that."

"Tell me about it."

"It can be forged into molded pieces to make tools. It is malleable. You can even make jewelry out of it." Gilbert examined his spoon thoughtfully.

"Is it valuable like gold?" she asked.

"Not exactly. Unlike gold, it can oxidize and lose its luster." Gilbert pointed over his shoulder. "I noticed you have interesting pieces on your mantel."

Madeleine glanced at the mantel. "You mean the medallion?"

"That and those rocks."

Madeleine and Gilbert rose and walked to the mantel.

"It's a fragment of metal," explained Madeleine.

Gilbert picked up the gray piece, which was sitting next to the big medallion display.

"This is a zinc ingot. It is exactly what I was talking about. Where did you get it?" He studied it carefully.

"I had almost forgotten," Madeleine said. "When I was a child, my father took me up the slope to the gray area. We found it there." Gilbert picked up the medallion.

"It's gold."

"The town issued it to my father, honoring him for the many structures he built."

"He's a lucky man. I have never had such an honor."

"That is not true. We are honored here to have you in our house."

"Let me take you to the gray area again. We can go by horseback."

"A horse back?"

"Yes, we ride on their backs."

"I have never done that."

"You can do it with ponies, too. Horses are stronger."

"It sounds like fun. Shall I prepare a lunch?"

"That would be nice of you. Shall we say at sunrise?"

"Sunrise," Madeleine said.

"With the roosters."

"I must check on my father. He's asleep in the chair again."

"Does he sleep a lot?"

"Most of the day."

"That's a lot."

"I am so afraid one day he won't wake up."

"You worry too much."

"I'll be right back." When she left the room he studied her cooking utensils. When she returned, Gilbert was standing near the door.

"I should go, it's late."

"It is," Madeleine said.

"Sunrise?"

"Sunrise."

"Good night."

"Good night."

CHAPTER 9

The next morning Gilbert opened his eyes to the warm rays of the sun streaking into the stable. He looked up through the cracks to see a new day sparkle to life. As he moved around in the wagon, the horses whickered softly. The big door swung open letting the sunlight flood the dirt floor. Madeleine approached the wagon carrying the basket that Gilbert had made for her. When she knocked on the wagon, Gilbert poked his head out.

"It contains fresh biscuits I made this morning." Her sparkling smile creased her gentle face. The wonderful aroma of the biscuits merged with the acute horse smell.

"You must be the angel of my dreams." Her smile broke even wider, and she bowed her head. Gilbert took one of the biscuits. He didn't take his eyes from her all the time he raised the morsel to his waiting lips. The first bite made him moan with delight.

"How did you make something so divine?" She shielded her eyes from the sun's strong rays.

"They're made with love."

"Well, then, I shall love them as well." Madeleine beamed with happiness. Larson whinnied and Nixon turned about and bobbed his head. Madeleine noticed the horse smell much more intensely. Gilbert slipped off the carriage seat, still chewing.

"Are you ready to ride on Larson's back?" he asked.

"I guess so." Gilbert pulled out a saddle and flung it over the animal's back. He grabbed Larson's mane, still holding the last of the bread in his teeth.

"Easy, there fellow. Easy boy." He fastened the strings and set up the bridle. The horse moved a little forward, then back.

"Now climb up on the wagon," he said, holding Larson. "You can use the wagon to help you get onto the horse."

She climbed up while Gilbert held the beast steady. Larson was very cooperative and gentle with Madeleine wiggling on his back. When she finally put all of her weight on him, the horse whinnied a little, as though clearing his throat. He took several steps back. Gilbert lifted the reins and handed them to Madeleine. "Just pull them back gently. The horse will know what you want to do." She pulled and Larson reared his head and stepped back. Gilbert grabbed the bridle, "C'mon, boy." The horse obeyed and Gilbert led him around in the stable.

"Nice ride," Madeleine said. "I feel I'm up so high."

"Just hold on to the horn."

"Like this?"

Then Gilbert saddled Nixon. He tied the basket to his horse and they left the stable together. The two horses swung their tails in concert as they walked along the cobblestone road until it turned into a dirt road. At the road's end, they cantered through the meadow until the slope became steep. They rested and talked for a few minutes. When they resumed, they slowly disappeared up the dirt path, leaving a trail of dust behind.

It took hours to reach the scree slopes of the mountain. They dismounted on the steep terrain and walked their animals up the slope, allowing them to carry their loads. When at last they stopped to rest, Madeleine looked down into the ravine and the Auguliere valley beyond. She took in a deep breath in the thin mountain air while Gilbert watched her.

"I never realized how beautiful it is up here," she said, twisting a twig. "You can see the entire village. I must have forgotten how much my father loved it here."

"There are many beauties in this vast world you are yet to see," Gilbert told her.

"One could never tell from this viewpoint that evil prevails down there."

"Evil always prevails in the world," Gilbert said. "We have to be strong to overcome it."

"Overcome it?" Madeleine said. "Really!" She sat among the edelweiss, allowing her faded blue dress to float all around her.

"Look, look out over the meadows," Gilbert said, crouching next to her. "Notice the white doves."

Madeleine reined in her sarcasm and looked down the slope, past the scree, over the meadows.

"Yes, I can see them," Madeleine said, putting a finger to her lip pensively. "It is almost as though I am seeing them for the first time." Gilbert smiled at her in the bright sunshine.

"There is so much good in the world, but you can only see it if you are willing to look beyond the evil."

"You have a way of making everything beautiful," Madeleine said, clutching her dress.

"Because I look at it with my heart."

"There were always doves in Auguliere," Madeleine said, softly, "but I never really saw them until you made me realize they were there." She looked at him in a new way now.

"Then take the advice of the dove and fly free."

"What about my father?"

"What about him?" Gilbert said. "Don't you have relatives who could take care of him?"

"I have two sisters on the North Slope. They have their own agendas. They left home long ago after mother died. They would not want to do it. Besides, father needs me."

"Others need you, too," Gilbert said.

"There are other evils besides man."

"I have heard a lot about people's fears in this alpine region," Gilbert said. "What is it that they fear so much where it is so beautiful?"

"They especially fear the night of the full moon."

"Of all the nights, to fear the moon?"

"It is not the moon they fear. It is what the moon represents."

"It symbolizes something evil?"

"It's worse than that. When the moon is full, it brings out certain predators."

"I have seen the mountain lion and he is something to fear. They are not known to attack a man."

"A man can stand up to a lion. Not to a pack of wolves."

"Wolves!" Gilbert said. "There are wolves in this region?"

"Many," Madeleine said. "How much farther is it?"

"Are you tired from our long journey or just curious?"

"No, just curious."

"It shouldn't be much farther. I wonder if I can get my wagon up here."

"There used to be an old carriage road that loggers used generations ago."

"Somehow I never pictured this town with loggers."

"There are many secrets here, Gilbert. You have to be careful what you do here."

"Why?"

"Did you ever see Mrs. Teivel?"

"Oh, yeah. The reader and advisor."

"She finds out things. Then she uses them against people. She's been known to cause trouble."

"Funny you said that. The first day I was in town I walked into her shop. I was going to ask for advice and she read me like a book."

"You see."

"She's creepy. Why does she speak in riddles?"

"Oh, yes," Madeleine said, "the riddles."

"I never thought much about what she said."

"You have to watch out for her. She has a weird way of putting things. Nobody trusts her."

"Really?"

"Well, maybe one . . ." Madeleine choked on a smile.

Gilbert stood and reached out with his hand to Madeleine. She took it and rose to her feet without taking her eyes from him. He put his big hand gently on her shoulder and asked, "Hungry?" She lifted her head to catch the mountain breeze in her face.

"The fresh air makes a person hungry," she said. They mounted their horses and started up the steep slopes.

"The gray area is just ahead. Let's have lunch on the big rock." He pointed to a huge outcropping in the hillside. In a few minutes, the horses stepped carefully on the slope. They dismounted on the gray soil. Gilbert retrieved the basket and they dined in the bright sunshine atop the alpine meadow on the rocky scree slope. During their meal, Gilbert picked up samples of ore and stuffed them in his saddlebags.

"You see," he said, holding up the gray sample for Madeleine to see. "This is what we call 'ore.'" Madeleine took the piece in her hand for further examination. "I shall bring my wagon on the carriage road and haul ore down to it. When I bring a load back to the shop I will show you how I smelt it."

Madeleine smiled happily. She leaned her head back onto Gilbert's lap and said nothing. Gilbert spread his big hand gently on her forehead, reassuring her that the world was safe.

"Maybe there can be trust in people after all," Madeleine said, smiling.

"Maybe," Gilbert said, returning a smile.

When the shadows of other outcroppings infringed on their site, they mutually decided to descend to the village. They returned to the stable by nightfall, quietly leading the horses in.

Chapter 10

The next morning Gilbert awoke early to fit the skylight in the frame he had assembled nights before. He stood on the top rung of the ladder he had built to assess the area he planned to place the skylight. He had purchased a pane of glass at a shop that cuts to order. Suddenly, the big stable door swung open, letting the fresh morning light splatter over the dirt floor. Gilbert struggled among the rafters to identify the intruder.

"Vladimir?" Gilbert called, shifting himself awkwardly on the ladder. "Is that you?"

"It's me," Vladimir said. "In the flesh." He flung his arms out as if to receive an embrace as he looked up at Gilbert. His black hair and beard were just the same as Gilbert had remembered them.

"It's so good to see you," Gilbert said, sensing his carefree attitude. Vladimir walked into the shadows, and continued to look up. Now Gilbert felt something was missing, even though he couldn't decide what it was.

"I see you found work." He spotted Gilbert near the ceiling, hanging onto a rafter's edge.

"A bit of work," Gilbert said, wiping his brow.

"Agafon says you felt a callin'," Vladimir said.

"Is that so?" Gilbert laughed. "A wee bit," Gilbert said, viewing Vladimir between the rungs.

"Indeed," Vladimir said, with a broad smile. "Madeleine's a fine callin'." Gilbert blushed.

"I'm just a tenant."

"All of Auguliere knows quite differently."

"It's not that way," Gilbert said as he shook his head.

"Just a tenant?" Vladimir said. "You have to do better than that, laddie." Gilbert chuckled, stepping back down the ladder. "What's going on up the ladder?" asked Vladimir.

"That's a skylight. Iakov always wanted it."

"He's lost the use of it."

"Some day I'll bring him to the shop, let him see what I've been up to."

"What you've been up to?" Vladimir said. "What might that be?"

"I've been fixing things."

"Making things . . ." Vladimir said. "It's no secret Madeleine sold a whole wagon full of toys to the children of Auguliere."

"I'm glad."

"Are you, now?" Vladimir said. "She came home with fifty rubles. That's more than most make in a week."

"That so?"

"Didn't you know she was struggling with her taxes?"

"She mentioned the landlord."

"I wonder if you'll ever get to see what kind of a man he really is."

"I look for the good in all men."

"Gilbert, my friend, for him, you'll have to look very hard."

"Might you give me a hand with the glass?"

"Surely."

"If you could hand up the rope." Gilbert pointed to a coil in the corner.

"Where'd you get this rope?" Vladimir examined it.

"I made it."

"I was afraid you'd say that."

"Is there a problem with that?"

"There could be," Vladimir said, grunting. "I noticed you've replaced the hinges on the big door so it closes now." Once Gilbert took hold of the rope, he threaded it through a pulley, which made the hauling easier. It had already been attached to the pane. Vladimir was surprised. Vladimir guided the pane up to Gilbert as he hoisted it.

"It is a strange way you placed the hinge in the wood, as though it were burned in, but without burn marks. Just how did you do that?"

"My father taught me to mortise."

"Mortise?" Vladimir said. "What a strange name to call it." He braced the glass in place while he anchored it with wooden fasteners.

"It's a technique to set the hinge into the wood," Gilbert said.

"I've noticed you have what appears to be zinc ore from the North Slope."

"May I ask where your wonderful dog is?" Vladimir looked at the ground with shame on his face. It was as though day had turned to night.

"No," Vladimir said, turning away.

"I'm sorry," Gilbert said. "I hope I have not offended you."

"It was an accident," Vladimir said.

"I once had a dog." Vladimir looked away. "He was my nightly companion. He was run down by a mule train."

"I'm sorry," Vladimir said. "I have to go." Vladimir turned abruptly, and headed for the door.

"Wait, Vladimir." He ran out of the stable before Gilbert could climb down.

That night Gilbert lay awake in his wagon, troubled, unable to sleep. He was disturbed by Vladimir's sudden departure. Then he remembered Mrs. Teivel.

This time, when he looked up through the new skylight, he noticed the full moon. He watched it without speaking. The silence was broken by a distinctive and mysterious howl.

Chapter 11

Early in the morning of the first of the month, Mr. Robertson walked along the path from his house to the village in brisk strides. He reached the first settlement on the west side of the village just as the sun began to sparkle over the horizon. The landlord raised his fragile finger in the chilly morning air to grab the big, zinc knocker. It clanked when he dropped it. He stood erect and ready at the door. The short man who came to the door had his hands sticky with glue, as any shoemaker would have. The old felt hat he wore was moth-eaten and stained. A discoloration indicated where he had handled the brim. He smiled with broken brown teeth. The landlord stood erect, waiting for the man to speak.

"Fine day today, even for a humble shoemaker," the short man said, looking up.

"Have you your taxes, sir?" the landlord said, his voice full of scorn.

"Yes, sir," the shoemaker said, digging into his ragged trousers' pockets. "I have six rubles."

"Six rubles," the landlord mused. He scratched between the strands of black beard. The shoemaker glanced up hopefully at the stern landlord, who had one eyebrow raised questioningly.

"Didn't make much of a profit this month, sir," the shoemaker said. "It's a sticky business, you know."

"Sticky, indeed," the landlord said with a smirk, continuing to evaluate the situation. He purposely spoke in a soothing tone, which surprised the shoemaker.

"That is adequate," the landlord said, absorbing all the shoemaker's gestures. He made a note in the tablet he carried and turned around toward the street.

The shoemaker's wife had crept up behind her husband, carrying a new basket. She strained to see the landlord as he walked away. She shook her head in disgust.

"Not even a thank you?" she mumbled.

The landlord was still close enough to hear her. He turned back, smacked his black cane sharply on the ground, keeping a rigid profile.

"Did you say something, Mrs. Polanski?" the landlord asked.

She shook her head from side to side, moved back timidly, hiding behind her husband. The landlord tried to spot her hiding in the dim doorway, but he didn't try very hard.

"No, no," she said in the shadows with a soft defensive voice.

"What's that?" the landlord snapped.

"No, sir!" she said, knowing better than to disagree with him.

"I see there is a new basket weaver here in town," the landlord smirked. The shoemaker's wife backed up, displaying a fearful expression. "Would that be this insidious carpenter?" She shrugged her shoulders and stepped back even further, pulling her husband with her.

"I don't know," the shoemaker said. "I only know shoes."

"That's all you should know," the landlord said, finally withdrawing from the shoemaker's domicile.

The landlord continued his tax collecting chores. He arrived at a large chicken farmer's residence. First, he examined the coops, paying particular attention to the new wood. The farmer walked up to him.

"Mornin'!" the farmer said, tipping his straw hat, holding his parka in the chilled morning air. The landlord pulled at his stringy beard.

"Twelve rubles, sir," the landlord said, glancing at notes he had jotted down on the tablet.

"But sir," the farmer whined. "It was ten rubles last month."

"The water table has been low. I have placed restrictions on water usage. I see you have been lavishing your coops with water." The landlord observed stacks of lumber. "What's all this new wood for?"

"But, Mr. Robertson," the farmer said, "'tis necessary to maintain my farm."

"'Tis necessary to maintain the village, Mr. Winthrop." The farmer reached into his pockets and found some coins. He dropped them in the landlord's dirty hand. "That is only four," the landlord said. He walked to the rear of the coops, where he noticed construction. "I also see you have new coops."

"The carpenter has built them," Mr. Winthrop said.

"I shall make a note of this. Perhaps I shall take five rubles more." He quickly jotted more notes on his tablet.

"I shall fetch a five ruble note from the residence, sir." The landlord waited, his manner restless, carefully examining the craftsmanship of the work, twitching one of the heavy eyebrows. He finally returned.

"I have eleven altogether."

"It'll have to do this month," the landlord said. "You had better pay me the back taxes before next month's taxes are due." The landlord straightened his hat, turned and started to walk away.

"Yes, sir," the farmer said, watching until the landlord disappeared in the morning haze.

In a couple of hours, he came to Madeleine's shanty. The knocker sounded. Madeleine was already awake, anticipating the landlord's arrival. She opened the door to the tall, thin man dressed in black.

"I have all the tax money." She extended her hand with the currency.

"Well, now," the landlord said, in his gruff voice. "It seems you can do it when you need to." The landlord left, counting the money to make sure it was complete.

He ambled on to the center of town, past the big well. Here, on a side street, a tiny shanty occupied the space next to a small stable. It belonged to Pavel and his mother, Oleg. The landlord hammered the knocker. Oleg came to the door sleepy-eyed. Pavel stood behind her, holding her leg.

"Have you the taxes you owe, my dear?"

"We had no income this month," Oleg said. "Our pony was sick and couldn't work," she pleaded. "You know I have no husband."

"Looks like you can afford toys."

"It was a gift of the carpenter."

"Why is this carpenter always involved in everyone's affaires?" the landlord screamed. "Who is this carpenter?"

"He seems to be a kind man."

"Kind?" the landlord shouted. "That's not a word I hear when things need to be done, young woman. Only the strong can lead. The weak perish.You still owe me three month's back taxes. Either produce the taxes or I shall have no alternative but to tear your shanty down."

Oleg regarded the ground, unable to look at Mr. Robertson. Pavel clung to his mother, saying, "Lan, lan," and hiding his face in her dress.

"I shall hear no more of this man. He'll rue the day he was born if he continues his 'deeds.'"

"Are you forbidding me to see him?" Oleg asked.

"I cannot forbid such a thing," he said. "I am monitoring your activities. You will let me know if you receive any more 'gifts.'"

Oleg looked away, implying she hoped the landlord would withdraw from her shanty. She turned her head to observe her son playing on the shanty floor behind her.

"I am not a woman in a position to receive gifts from a man," Oleg said.

"Actually," the landlord said. "You are not much of a woman to look at, let alone have a man look at you." She bowed her head in his presence.

"I am a woman, and one of honor."

"Your honor is written all over your ability to keep up with your obligations, which has proved to be doubtful." She took part of her dress to wipe her eyes. "Look at you!" He stepped back into the street with a display of disgust.

"Why don't you treat Madeleine like that?" Oleg said. "Is it because she has a father?"

"You are pathetic. Clean yourself up, woman!"

He turned toward the street again, and departed, leaving Oleg with too much to think about. Although her friendship with Madeleine was shaky at best, Oleg needed to have Madeleine believe in her. Unlike Madeleine, Oleg did not even have a father to talk to. While Madeleine was very independent, Oleg teetered on the verge of collapse ever since her husband had died. She tried to believe it was just an accident, but Madeleine had told her she suspected something menacing since the landlord had happened to be at the construction site that day.

The landlord walked past Madeleine's shanty again, this time peeking into the stable he thought was abandoned.

Although Gilbert was not in the shop, the landlord delighted in observing all the equipment he possessed, and studied all of his work with curiosity.

"Hm!" he mused. "It would seem to me this carpenter has established a commercial residence here. I will have to look into what kind of rental obligation he should have. As far as my dear Madeleine is concerned, she will have to uphold the burden of the additional tax." He smiled to himself. "Tomorrow shall be a day of inquisition."

Chapter 12

Madeleine was alone in Gilbert's shop early the next morning when Mr. Robertson arrived. Gilbert had ridden on horseback with Larson to the alpine barrens to look for wood. The landlord took advantage of the opportunity to learn something about the carpenter. He stepped near Nixon, but the animal reared back and neighed.

"Dumb animal," the landlord rattled. He spotted Madeleine at Gilbert's worktable; then he leered over his shoulder at the wagon's sign. He cleared his throat, causing Madeleine to take notice.

"Tell me a little something about this Gilbert O'Sullivan," the landlord bellowed.

Madeleine grinned with nervous anticipation. She watched Nixon step back.

"What do you want to know?" she said, looking over Gilbert's plans. As the landlord advanced, she saw his intimidating face. Madeleine hunched over the worktable, pretending to be absorbed.

"What is he building?"

Madeleine regarded him with suspicion, even though she knew he was nosey. He maintained a cold sneer on his face, still glancing at Nixon on occasion.

"He has a shop here," Madeleine confided, folding the plans and standing up straight.

"Don't patronize me, Miss Knesnovich."

He turned completely around, letting his cane strike the dirt floor.

"He makes tools and toys," Madeleine said, wiping her dainty brow.

"Out of wood?" the landlord said. He took out his tablet, scribbled information on it, and peeked at Madeleine's face.

"Well, he's a carpenter," she said.

The landlord pulled his lips together to form a tight seal, and drew his eyebrows close. He adjusted his top hat and stepped back. He looked down again at his tablet, ready to write new items on it.

"Where does he get this wood from?"

Madeleine gulped, facing him squarely. Fear surged through her body as she regarded his cold demeanor.

"He uses aspen wood, I think." She put one hand over the other, crossed her ankles, and stood in front of the papers with terrifying thoughts.

"Oh, he uses the aspen trees from the park?" Mr. Robertson smirked knowingly. He stared at Madeleine from across the table.

"I don't know," Madeleine said, shaking. "I never saw where he gets them." She shook her head negatively. She sucked in her lips, shuffling her feet where she stood.

"My grandfather planted those trees."

"I . . . I didn't know that . . ." She drew in a full breath.

"That's good," the landlord said.

"It is?" Madeleine said, taking in another gulp of air.

The landlord stepped back, letting his beady eyes survey the shop.

"It is," he said, letting out a breath.

"Oh," Madeleine said. "I hadn't realized."

"There's an abundance of them now," the landlord admitted. "Thinning them out is better for their growth."

He surprised Madeleine, but she remained cautious. She considered that the landlord was trying to trap her into admitting what Gilbert was up to. She had to remain on guard. She knew how devious he could be.

"Oh, yes," Madeleine thought, slightly relieved, "I guess it is."

She continued to feel suspicious, despite his condoning tree thinning. She brushed her hair back, feeling awkward standing in front of Gilbert's plans. She felt a need to protect them from the landlord's view.

"What is it you want from Gilbert's shop?" Madeleine bravely said. He thought for a moment, bringing his hands together.

"Have you sold the shop to this carpenter?"

"No, I haven't. He pays me rent."

"Oh, really?" he said in a brisk tone.

"It's only a modest sum." Madeleine gulped again, stepping slightly back.

"Not for long," the landlord said. Madeleine's fears were realized now. The landlord seemed to be claiming her father's property with his eyes. She pressed her lips together, anger evident in her eyes. She felt violated.

"According to my records, Miss Madeleine Knesnovich, this property has owed back taxes for years." Madeleine swallowed, struggling with the import of his message. She tried to recall what part of the taxes had been paid. She never remembered her father even mentioning it. He smiled victoriously.

"Whatever taxes he owes," Madeleine promised, "I shall pay." The landlord maintained a rigid stance and never flinched as he watched Madeleine's quivering hands.

"You won't be able to manage that."

"Why not?" Madeleine was left in a state of agitation to which she was unaccustomed.

"It is substantially beyond you, my dear," the landlord assured. "Your father never paid them. It goes back for years."

Now Madeleine felt a sharp pang of fear shooting up her spine. She gripped the worktable as though bracing for impact. Her eyes grew red and swelled with tears.

"So, what are you saying?" Madeleine said, in her quivering voice. The landlord reveled in Madeleine's desperate expression, with a drawn out, dastardly smile.

"I'm afraid I will have to foreclose on it," he said, with callous delight.

His sharp words reached all the way to her heart as though she were struck in the chest with an arrow. Madeleine stood, wobbling to the point of collapse, as the feeling absorbed her weakening body.

"Mr. O'Sullivan will be paying me the rent from now on," the landlord said in an aloof state.

Madeleine stepped back and shook her head in disbelief, dropping her jaw. She felt panic-stricken and trapped when she realized her desperate state.

"You can't do that," she said, pausing to search the ground, thinking of her income. "It'll, it'll . . ."

"Put a little strain on your budget?" he said.

Madeleine continued to look down, letting her eyelids droop. She kicked some dirt crumbs around. Nixon shook his head, thrashing his gorgeous mane. The animal dropped some dung, and urinated on the dirt floor, emitting a powerful horse odor.

"My father . . ." she began.

"My father . . ." the landlord mimicked.

Madeleine was no longer able to control the flow of tears, which filled her eyes like basins. She fumbled at the bench with Gilbert's plans. She felt the true pressure of the dilemma. On the one hand, she hoped Gilbert would suddenly appear to support her. On the other hand, she didn't want Gilbert to see her so vulnerable. Only the horse would know the truth and he seemed to comfort her. She looked up at him for a minute, thinking she would find a way to retaliate against the landlord for hurting her so much.

"Get hold of yourself, girl," he insisted. Madeleine looked away from him, choking on her words. Finally, she ran out of the stable in an emotional turmoil. Then the landlord, with a malevolent smile, left, having finished his job.

Chapter 13

The landlord returned the next morning to find Gilbert working in his shop. Pavel was also present. The landlord strutted into the stable like an owner. Whenever he entered any shop the owners were always on guard, fearing retaliation for any attempt to defend their property. Gilbert didn't appear to be moved by the landlord's appearance. He gazed up at him from his work and smiled cordially.

"You'll be paying the rent to me from now on," the landlord said, briskly. "I don't know what you paid Miss Knesnovich, but I get fifty rubles for the use of this shop. Is that clear, young man?"

"What right do you have to come into Madeleine's shop and speak so strongly to me?"

"What right do I have?" the landlord said. "You have the audacity to demand to know my rights?" Gilbert shrank back from the landlord's acrid accusations.

"Yes," Gilbert ventured to say.

"Who are you, a stranger to Auguliere, who dare ask about my rights?"

"Madeleine owns this stable . . ." The landlord laughed, with a big "hah," defying Gilbert.

With Pavel holding onto one of his legs tightly, Gilbert stood confused and unsure. Mr. Robertson's bold remarks prevented him from thinking logically.

"Wait a minute," Gilbert acquired the nerve to say.

"I have all the rights," the landlord announced. "I own the property now." Gilbert swallowed, regarding the landlord's eyes, as though flares emanated from them. "Is that clear?" the landlord said.

"Yes," Gilbert struggled to say, clearing his throat.

"I can't hear you," the landlord fired.

"Yes, sir!" Gilbert yelled, with a slight gurgle in his voice.

"Having trouble with your speech, Mr. O'Sullivan?"

"No," Gilbert whispered.

"What's that?"

"No, sir!" Gilbert shouted.

"Now that we have our misunderstanding all cleared up, we can conduct business."

"Yes, sir!"

"I'll take the first payment now."

"Now?"

"Rent is due with the new moon, on the first of the month," the landlord said.

"That's today," Gilbert said.

"Isn't that a coincidence," the landlord smirked.

Gilbert reached into his pocket, counted out money and handed it to the landlord.

"I'll see you next month," the landlord said, with finality.

The landlord had conducted cold business with no gratitude or farewell. Gilbert found himself challenged to find the good in this human being. He reflected in anguish for a long moment on Vladimir's words of warning. Then, his mind clouded, he forced himself to retreat. He didn't know Madeleine watched from the safety of the window.

He hitched up the horses and headed to the pine barrens. Although he felt plagued by the turn of events, he had to continue his work, aware that much still needed to be done.

Gilbert came back late that night with a wagon full of pine logs and pine resin. Madeleine had been peeking from her kitchen window for the flicker of Gilbert's lamp. When she at last spied him, she sprang from her shanty while Gilbert unloaded his wagon. She approached him carefully so he would not be startled. Gilbert looked up from the wagon bed.

"Now what'd be on a fine maiden's mind on a cold and clammy night?"

"The landlord came by yesterday, while you were out." She gazed at the ground thoughtfully, stroking Larson. The horse reacted by bobbing his big head. Madeleine sniffed the acrid horse smell.

"I happened to be in the shop."

"So?"

"So, he pressured me."

"Did he hurt you?"

"No. He didn't hurt me. Well, in a way he did."

"How?"

"Well, not physically."

"Now this is getting cryptic."

"I'm sorry. You're the last person I should burden with this."

"Why do you feel it's a burden to me?"

"It means I won't be able to ask a rental from you." Her eyes had filled with tears. He stood erect and speechless, not knowing how to answer, although he became acutely aware of Madeleine's vulnerability.

"We will find a way around this."

"You don't understand," Madeleine said. "I don't want to burden you with my troubles. You must have plenty of your own."

"Actually, I don't." She looked at him strangely and wondered how he could not have any troubles. *Everybody has troubles,* she thought.

"You are never a burden to me." It was as though he had a way of absorbing all the hurt and sorrow she felt.

"I can't understand how you could stand there, with the weight of all your troubles and not allow them to affect you."

"They affect me, Madeleine," Gilbert assumed. "I try to contain them so they don't spill over into other people's lives."

"You do have a way of turning everything around."

"I'm not trying to make you feel bad."

"That's just it. You have this way of putting things. You make people feel everything's going to be fine. You make people feel secure."

"Why not make them feel that way?"

"The world is not secure. No one is safe. Isn't that false hope?"

"No. False hope would be misleading people. Have I done that?"

"No."

"I can give people a chance to see things a different way."

"You see, there you go again," she sobbed.

The door opened, letting someone inside the stable. Madeleine was alerted to the intruder. When he came near to the light, she recognized him. "Vladimir?" Vladimir smiled, reaching for Madeleine's hand. He squeezed her hand gently. Madeleine let out a deep breath.

"It's so good to see you," Vladimir said. He turned toward Gilbert, "It's good to see you, too, Gilbert." Gilbert nodded. Madeleine appeared to be looking for something around Vladimir.

"What's the matter, Maddy?" he said.

"Seems like something's missing."

"Missing?" Vladimir said. It suddenly occurred to her.

"Where's Chipper, Vladimir?" Madeleine said. Gilbert shook his head at Madeleine, trying to stop her from asking the question.

"How about some tea?" Gilbert suggested, interrupting Madeleine. "I made it fresh." Madeleine saw that Gilbert was getting nervous. Vladimir didn't answer right away, as though he were trying to decide whether or not to tell them about Chipper.

"Chipper's busy tonight," Vladimir finally said.

Gilbert looked surprised. He cleared his throat and stepped back to get the tea. Madeleine thought Vladimir was hiding something and wondered why. She felt reluctant to tell Gilbert what she really knew. When Gilbert returned, Vladimir was already sitting in one of Gilbert's handmade chairs.

"Nice chair," Vladimir said

"Thank you. Here's tea," Gilbert said.

"Gilbert's very industrious," Vladimir said to Madeleine, alluding to the skylight by motioning with his eyes. Turning to Gilbert, he said, "I see you got it in." Gilbert looked up at it and shrugged his shoulders.

"When the sun comes out, the whole shop is illuminated," Gilbert said, turning toward Madeleine, who also assumed a seat in one of Gilbert's chairs. "Hope Iakov can see it soon." Madeleine bowed her head and looked down. Vladimir let his eyes flit back and forth between them.

"Is there something you two are keeping from me?" Vladimir said.

"Yes," Gilbert said. "There is."

Gilbert's implication bothered Madeleine. She couldn't imagine what Gilbert was keeping from Vladimir. Her eyes started to moisten as the landlord came into her mind, making her hands shake. Even Vladimir somehow noticed.

"You were about to tell me about Chipper, I believe," Madeleine said. Vladimir looked down to the barn floor.

"Yes, Chipper," Vladimir said. "I don't know where to begin."

"Something happened to Chipper?" Madeleine surmised.

"It was an accident," Vladimir said. "Can't we just forget it?"

"Yes, we can," Gilbert said, defending Vladimir. Madeleine shook her head in disagreement. Gilbert turned toward her, lifting his tea. "It's better to leave Vladimir be. He's been through enough." Vladimir looked up to Gilbert gratefully.

"I am sorry, Vladimir," Madeleine said.

"It's late," Vladimir said. "I have to get back. Don't worry about it. What's done is done."

"If you ever need a friend . . ." Gilbert promised.

"I know," Vladimir said. "Here, too."

He consumed his tea, stood and planted his hat comfortably on his head. He waved and walked out. Gilbert and Madeleine were left to wonder.

"I have never seen him so troubled," Madeleine observed.

"Now you know," Gilbert said.

"I don't mean about the dog," Madeleine said. "There's something else bothering him. We can't do anything about it."

Gilbert had a renewed look of concern. He searched Madeleine's face as though he could find what was there. It was obvious to Madeleine that he struggled to see beyond her flesh, to ferret out what was bothering her deep in her heart. The harder he looked, the more bewildered he became, and Madeleine could sense it.

"It's late, Gilbert," Madeleine finally said. "I should tend to my father."

"I understand, Madeleine. Go, tend to him."

He stood, stepping back to allow her to rise. She also finished the last of her tea. She took his hand, putting the cup down with the other hand.

"I'm glad you're in Auguliere," she said, as he smiled warmly.

"So am I."

She smiled again and slowly walked out of the barn. When she returned to her shanty, she lit her candle. Gilbert saw it from the window. He picked up his ax and chopped some wood. Madeleine heard the chopping and wondered what he was doing. She made sure her father was comfortable before she climbed into her own bed. After her candle went out, Gilbert put the fresh-cut wood on her doorstep before retiring for the night.

Chapter 14

A rumble shook Madeleine's bed until it awakened her. She jumped up from her dreams and let her feet search the floor for her slippers. She heard Iakov whimper, indicating the noise disturbed him as well.

"What is it, father?" she called from her room. Madeleine glanced between the open doors of both rooms to see that he was trying to sit up to listen better.

"I know that sound," he said, pushing against the bed with his hands as hard as he could. "That is the sound of hooves on the dirt in the street."

"What does it mean?" Madeleine said, stumbling to her feet, reaching her father's room, still in her nightgown.

"Animals in large numbers are running together," he said, finally propping himself in a sitting position. "Listen." Madeleine studied his contorted face. She saw expressions on it unfamiliar to her. "You had better get dressed."

"Why, father?" she said looking at him in a dazzled state. "What's wrong?"

He shook his head from side to side, tension visible in his eyes, and looked down at the covers. He fell back into the pillow on the bed, looking up at the ceiling.

Madeleine obeyed him and ran back to her room to get dressed.

"Why?" she asked her father again, calling to him from her room. A long silence pervaded the air.

"I heard this before," he finally said, in a throaty voice. She reentered his room, now fully dressed. He looked up at her with renewed concern.

"Please tell me, father." She gaped at him, knowing full well he had the answers.

"It is the sound of an organized group, controlled by a man."

"The landlord!" Madeleine surmised. "I want to warn Gilbert. He doesn't know what the landlord's capable of. He may think something's happened to the village, like an earthquake."

"No, Madeleine," Iakov said. "It is too dangerous. Gilbert can take care of himself." They both heard a loud crash. It sounded like a tornado had struck the village, even though the day was bright and sunny. Madeleine could not control herself any longer. The sound's strangeness compelled her to investigate.

"Madeleine!" her father nervously called. "Madeleine!" It was too late. Madeleine had opened the door and tripped over the woodpile left the night before.

"Who left this here?" she thought. "Oh, what a bad time for it!"

She picked herself up, assessed her bruises, pulled her pride together, brushed her dress down and journeyed into the empty early morning streets of Auguliere amid the horrendous sounds that were generated. As she ran through the streets, she saw a giant cloud of dust rising over the tops of buildings in the area behind her father's stables. Whom did she know from this region? She could not recall anyone. Still, concern drove her to find out. If this was connected in any way with the landlord, it would fortify her anger.

Madeleine walked briskly through the streets checking each alleyway, hoping not to find an impending disaster. Every time she peered up a side street, she cringed. When she finally turned up the broad street near the market, she could see the dust billowing out from between structures. The dust intensified as she walked towards it, quickening her pace. Her heart thumped harder as she moved. When she finally reached the street, the reality was too overwhelming. She drew her hand up against her mouth and gasped. The scene was like a nightmare. She could not even identify the remnants of the shanty. Wood was splintered and strewn all over. First, she searched the rubble with her eyes twitching frantically. No human life stirred.

As the dust settled, she saw a large open wagon roll by on the main street with a team of mules, drawn by a thin man in a black suit with a top hat.

A sick feeling persisted in her stomach as she surveyed the scene, walking closer to the fragments of what had been a shanty. Luckily, the nearby stable hadn't been knocked down, and the resident animal was not hurt. She began to rummage through the debris, hoping not to find anyone. She found little reminders that this place had been occupied—a blanket, a smashed teakettle, a knife, a spatula, and some torn and dirty garments. She recognized one of the garments as Oleg's.

Madeleine sat down on a piece of rubble, feeling exhausted and defeated, permitting the events of the last ten minutes to occupy her thoughts. She grappled with questions of whether or not Oleg survived the attack on her shanty, as she gaped at the broken skin on her knuckles from her fall. She knew the landlord was evil, but she couldn't imagine he would destroy someone's house. A dry sob escaped her throat, as she feared for the missing shanty dwellers.

Then, breaking the persistent silence, a voice spoke behind her. In another second, Pavel appeared. Madeleine turned and stood. She grabbed him with both her arms, hugging him, and not letting him go.

"I'm glad you're safe," she said. Pavel smiled and pointed behind her.

"Ma," he said, pointing, as Madeleine turned her head. Pavel's mother stood amid the rubble. She was not hurt, but she kept her head down as she moved nearer. She spoke in a soft tone, unlike the tone of a victim. Yet Madeleine witnessed the hurt etched over Oleg's weathered face.

"I feel sorry for Mr. Robertson," Oleg said.

"Sorry?" Madeleine inquired, stunned by Oleg's words.

"He's a lonely man. He doesn't understand love and tenderness. He won't ever see a son of his own."

"He has perseverance," Madeleine said. "Come back to my shanty where you can have tea and sit with my father and me."

"You are kind."

"Wasn't love promised in Auguliere?" The woman regarded her worn out shoes and pulled at her ragged dress. It was as though a tear wanted to form in her eye, but was too dry to form. She glanced at her son with a smile.

"I hope he will grow up to be a man of honor."

"He will, with love." The two women returned to Madeleine's shanty. Iakov was sitting in his chair by then, having wheeled himself into the kitchen.

"Father, I brought Oleg and Pavel back. They . . ."

"I know," Iakov surmised. "Mr. Robertson came to collect." Oleg bowed her head and Madeleine shrugged.

"Madeleine," he said, "Better fetch some water down at the well if you want to make tea."

"I'll do it!" The sound of the young, robust voice at the door startled the women. Pavel also turned, to see Gilbert's smiling face. Iakov beamed. Oleg looked back and forth between Pavel and Gilbert. You could see the connection in their facial expressions. Camaraderie was apparent. Pavel immediately stood.

"Gil, Gil!" he tried to say, and Gilbert extended his big hand to the boy. Pavel took it and held onto it with his two hands. The women looked at each other without saying anything. Iakov smiled. Gilbert picked up the pail, and the two of them left, leaving both women baffled.

"That man has a powerful effect on Pavel," Oleg acknowledged, once Gilbert was gone.

"Yes," Madeleine said, "I know. He has that effect on a lot of people in Auguliere."

"I wonder why that is," Oleg said.

"I'll never forget the first time I saw him. He seemed to put the whole world back in order. Whatever problems lurked in Auguliere, he seemed to have the answer. I believed there was nothing Gilbert O'Sullivan couldn't do."

"You really summed it up," Oleg said.

"What really made me happy was to see the town reborn," Madeleine said.

"There's an evil side to Auguliere," Oleg said.

"I know," Madeleine admitted.

"All this goodness comes with a price," Oleg said. "There is something to fear in Auguliere. There is one wicked man who will find a way to take it all down, a man to defy the very meaning of decency. This scares me to death."

Minutes later Gilbert and Pavel returned with the water for tea. Gilbert came into the shanty and placed the heavy pail on the kitchen counter. Madeleine glowed with happiness. She felt all his goodness was directed to her alone.

"You deserve a really good and hot tea," Madeleine said. Oleg observed her work, her eyebrows knit in pain. She sat quietly like a dog with her tail drawn between her legs.

Madeleine made the tea for everyone. She lovingly poured the hot tea into each of the waiting cups. The steam billowed in the air like miniature smoke stacks. They all sipped the steaming beverage, puckering their lips to protect them from the heat.

"I have traveled widely," Gilbert began, when Madeleine had settled down next to him. *To what interesting places had Gilbert traveled*, she wondered to herself.

"I have been to the deep south of the country, where it is forever warm." Oleg glanced at Pavel and grinned, while Gilbert continued. "They have citrus fruit on their trees. The peel of the fruit gives wonderful oil that flavors the tea." Gilbert impressed Madeleine with his knowledge once again. She reclined in the chair, holding her cup firmly between her palms, looking thoughtfully into the tea.

"Hm!" Madeleine mused. "An oil that flavors tea . . ."

"There are other strange fruits that do not grow in the hills of Auguliere."

Oleg took her cup to her lips, looking up to see Madeleine's brows rise.

"In the south, the family usually helps build a new shanty," Gilbert broached the subject awkwardly.

"Oleg, what will you do?" Madeleine asked with concern.

Oleg bowed her head, holding Pavel close. Madeleine set her cup down during Oleg's silence. Gilbert faced Madeleine, as she pushed her chair away from the table.

"Why don't I just build a room for her and Pavel?" Gilbert said. Oleg's jaw dropped. She stared at Gilbert, blinking her eyes, unbelieving.

"Build a room?" Madeleine asked. "Just like that?"

"It would be easy for me," Gilbert assured. "There is so much room in the barn, as long as you don't mind horses," he said, turning to Oleg. "I hope you understand I cannot send them outside at night."

Oleg still didn't know how to answer. She shook her head slightly as she listened to Gilbert. She smiled for the first time.

"I understand," she said. She whisked back her dusty hair.

"What about uncle Petrenko?" Madeleine suggested, studying Oleg's face diligently. She recalled his distinct appearance.

"He is too intoxicated with spirits," Oleg said.

"That's Petrenko." She turned back to Gilbert, who sat quietly, waiting for a response.

"I remember as a child," Oleg began. "He was my dearest uncle. I can still remember the ride he gave me on his pony."

"Where is he now?" Madeleine asked.

"He did things I'm not proud of. The landlord's been after him."

"I remember him stealing father's corn." Madeleine said.

"The landlord tried to have him hanged. Maybe he's not a good influence on Pavel," Oleg admitted.

"No," Madeleine said. "I guess not."

"I gave life to my son. He needs the shelter that you are so kind to offer."

"It is the least I can do," Gilbert said. "Who could not open his home to you and your son?" Madeleine blinked her eyes rapidly.

"You will be blessed for your kindness," Oleg assured. "I will pray for you." Madeleine turned away from Oleg, knitting her brows in thought.

"Retrieve as many things as you can from your shanty," Gilbert insisted. "Bring them to the barn. I will move the storage of wood."

"Why don't you store it in my stable? My pony won't mind. That's the only thing the landlord left standing."

"Thanks."

Oleg stood, brushing her soiled dress gently, making clouds of dust appear as she walked past Madeleine, and out of the shanty. Madeleine regarded her with her head down as she passed. Now Madeleine gave Gilbert her full attention. Pavel dropped down to the wood floor and played with the chair legs.

"You are too kind."

"I have to do what needs to be done."

"I see."

"It is only right."

"Of course, you must do what's right."

Madeleine realized perhaps all his goodness was not directed specifically at her. It made her feel uncomfortable. She felt that something strange was happening to her, something she clearly didn't understand. When Oleg returned, Gilbert saw her in a distressed state.

"The landlord is so evil. How could he do this?" She held the remnants of her water buckets in her hands.

"I can make you new ones," Gilbert said.

"I have no way to pay you," Oleg said. Madeleine only gawked at Oleg.

"You don't have to pay me," Gilbert said. "Besides, Pavel helps me around the shop. I should pay him a wage."

"I noticed he looks up to you as a big brother." Madeleine watched Oleg and Gilbert with an indifferent expression pasted on her face.

"I never had a little brother."

That afternoon Pavel helped Gilbert fabricate the walls in the corner of the stable for the new room. That job took most of the day. Gilbert had just hauled several aspen logs into the shop. Pavel stood near watching Gilbert work on them, trimming the edges with his ax. Several hours later, he erected the first studs for the walls. He used thin boards that he had cut on his mill for completing the walls. They were held in place with wooden pegs he fastened into holes he had drilled. The wall was held together by the frame's grooves. Oleg watched with fascination. When he was done, he wove strands of aspen bark across a rectangular frame he had made earlier. This formed a grid. Pavel had collected several wool blankets from the wreckage to make a bed for Oleg. Pavel would sleep in the extra bed in the shop, and Gilbert would continue to sleep in the wagon.

When the walls were complete, he laid out some strips for a door. Gilbert used his metal hinges for the door.

Madeleine returned to the shop that evening with hot supper.

"I must be in heaven," Gilbert said. Madeleine laughed. Pavel looked up to Gilbert proudly as Oleg regarded Madeleine with envy.

"You work too hard," Madeleine said.

"I only do what needs to be done."

"Indeed you do," Oleg said with a sarcastic tone.

"I have some bricks and some mortar," Gilbert said, "If Pavel could find your grate, perhaps, I can build a firebox for your cooking."

Madeleine blinked her eyes with a frowning expression.

"My father needs me," she said. She picked up her basket and left.

"Why are you so good?" Oleg asked. She gave Gilbert a meaningful look.

"Go, Pavel," Oleg said. "Find mommy's grate for the hearth." Pavel smiled and ran out.

Now Gilbert and Oleg were alone. Madeleine watched them from her window. Gilbert piled the heavy bricks in a wheelbarrow and rolled them into Oleg's room. She watched him unload the bricks.

"You are very strong," Oleg remarked. Gilbert didn't answer as he continued hauling the materials. She looked at him and she smiled with her eyes half closed.

"Are you feeling well?" Gilbert said.

"Never felt better."

"I thought you were looking at me strangely."

She moved away from the hearth site and sat on the bed.

"I was."

Gilbert poured some water into a pan filled with dry mortar. He mixed it with a trowel he had made from the aspen. She continued to watch him with fascination.

"Is something wrong?"

"Can't I watch a strong man work without having something wrong?"

"I guess so."

Madeleine couldn't see inside the room from her window. She believed more than brick-laying was going on. She slammed the window down angrily and marched into her room.

"Madeleine," her father called, "is everything all right?"

"Just fine, father," she said, hiding her shaky voice from him.

She approached the room, trying to cast aside the pleasant memories of their horseback ride. A new emotion found its way to her consciousness and she protested it loudly.

Chapter 15

The landlord woke up agitated. The thick morning fog had obscured his view when he tried to look out his window. He fumbled for his eyepiece as he mumbled to himself, "I have to find a way to stop this ogre from destroying Auguliere." He marched around in pajamas, searching the big house for his black trousers and white shirt.

"Maybe I left them in the armoire," he said. He walked to it, finding them draped neatly over the polished wood door.

"I must have hot tea before my arduous journey to the village." He stuffed the hearth with kindling and hay, and ignited the pile with flint. In minutes, the fire came to life.

"Here, I must contemplate; I shall think of a way to snare this carpenter. How shall I do it? First, let me warm my spirits with tea." The cat jumped onto his lap when he sat, purring loudly. "Produce your purr, sweet kitty. It shall be a reminder to me who will be the benefactor of Auguliere. Make no mistake, my feline friend," he pointed, "I shall prevail."

He stood, releasing the cat, then stepped closer to the hearth, stoking the fire, rubbing his hands together to keep them warm. "No beast nor man shall stop me from taking that which rightfully belongs to only me. All is mine by default," he said, stroking the animal's soft fur.

He picked up the kettle as it whistled and poured the hot beverage. He let his hands receive the steam, which radiated heat from the cup. The cat settled at his feet. "Hot tea always leaves my spirits in fine fettle." He walked through the house, admiring his lofty possessions. He stopped short at a shelf with a talisman. He picked it up. It brought back memories. "Mrs. Teivel." This prompted him to say aloud, "I shall go to her . . ."

He looked up at the divine trinket, admiring it with special appreciation.

"She will have the answers I seek," he said to the cat.

In another hour, he had hitched the mules to the wagon. Now he realized he had a purpose. He drove his wagon into town. When the wagon arrived at the street, he halted the team, stepped off the rig and tied the animals to the post. By now, the fog had started to lift, but the air was still murky and dank. He made his way to Mrs. Teivel's shop. The shabby curtains were drawn, and the place looked dark. When he tried the door, however, it opened easily. Once inside, he let the spring pull it shut.

The door had barely closed when she looked up. Her face reacted mechanically. Mrs. Teivel quickly stood to acknowledge the landlord. She was totally silent, as though she already knew what was on his mind. He stood in front of the counter like a man with a problem. When the woman spoke, her speech was checked by her predetermined knowledge.

"The way of the wood be on your mind. A carpenter's trait is hard to find."

"I am afraid of the irreparable damage this carpenter can do to Auguliere," the landlord confessed.

"Strength and character dominate your fear, a remedy is always near." The landlord allowed a timid smile to pervade his stiff expression.

"I am the rightful heir to all the wealth of Auguliere. I have tried to extinguish him by foreclosure of his shop, water restrictions to stop his works, destruction of the speech-impaired boy's shanty, and still he overcomes these obstacles."

She looked at him with the good eye, pounding her fists on the counter. "Do your deed, get your man . . . take the devil's contraband. Take your time, wait and see. One hundred rubles belong to me."

"One hundred rubles?" She stared at him relentlessly, with the good eye, unmoving, making him step back.

"Either you pay or the carpenter shall play." He grumbled, pushing his lips together and gritting his broken teeth. He reached deep into the slovenly suit's pockets for the currency. From a purse in his garment, he counted out one hundred rubles in paper notes. He maintained an angry sneer and continued to grumble as he handed over the money.

Mrs. Teivel grabbed it like a hungry lizard, quickly counting it and stashing it in her cleavage.

She turned and stepped up on a ladder. She reached up to the highest shelf and pulled out a filthy old jar with something black moving inside. When she returned to the counter, the landlord strained to see the contents of the odd container, barely visible through the dingy film that had collected on the glass over the years. She poured out something into a smaller, flat vessel, and placed it in his waiting hands. The landlord stared at the creatures with curiosity.

"With these beetles that I give . . . let them multiply to live." She smiled with contentment. "Put them in the aspen trees, where they mingle with the bees." She closed the landlord's hand and said, "Softening the wood's their deadly deed, preventing the growth in the carpenter's seed." The landlord stood frozen, a flicker of understanding on his face. When Mrs. Teivel returned to her chair, the landlord turned, gloating, and exited the shop.

The landlord drove his team to the town center, where he strolled into the park. Many of the older women who frequented the park were surprised to see the landlord lingering. Some turned their heads so as not to be recognized. The inhabitants of Auguliere always feared the landlord would suddenly ask for tax money anywhere and at any time; consequently, they shunned him. Mr. Robertson had a different agenda. Some women reported the landlord appeared as though he were enjoying the flowers and the plants by taking in the fragrance of their bouquet. Some saw this as a suspicious move. They speculated about what he was up to. They couldn't see his devious plan as he kept the beetles concealed. He didn't intend to frighten anyone or cause a scene.

In the park, the moment he released the creatures, they scampered away with remarkable speed, faster than he thought them capable, crawling up the bark and into the trees. They totally disappeared from sight almost instantly. When people saw him near the trees, they were too late to see his ambitious plan. No one saw any trace of insects. When the landlord saw his deed had been carried out, he smiled victoriously, and quietly left the park.

He rode to Madeleine's stable. Neither Madeleine nor Gilbert was around. The wagon was gone and the landlord knew Madeleine, Oleg and Pavel were in the market. The landlord saw his chance. No one saw him enter the barn. He strode up to the giant rack of toys and tools. He opened the flat container and allowed several beetles to escape onto the rack. They fled among the wooden toys. Once he had released them all, they scampered away, not to be seen again, until . . .

Chapter 16

Several days passed. Madeleine began to allay her fears. She felt that whatever the situation between Gilbert and Oleg, she could depend on his support no matter what. For the first time in years, she was truly carefree. She went about her business with a smile on her face. She made sure she came into daily contact with everyone who was important to her.

Madeleine's visits to the park had become part of her routine. Late in the afternoon on a beautiful day, Madeleine went to the park to watch the children play with toys Gilbert had made. Before Gilbert's presence, the commons area was always empty. Now, women came to sit amidst the fresh foliage to let their children play stone and stick games in the grass; and between the tall aspen trees, they played hiding games. Of course, there were now fewer trees since the carpenter had been felling them. The women also came to sit under the trees and gossip while nursing their babies. Many brought their small dogs. The dogs ran freely and played chase games. The children frolicked in the lazy shadows of the aspen trees. Mothers talked about life in Auguliere. An aura of happiness prevailed.

A woman came to the grounds with her boy, and sat on the bench next to Madeleine. She wore a contented face, admiring the carpenter's craftsmanship in the toy with which the child played. Madeleine saw the child moving one of the doll's arms when she noticed that something didn't seem right. It appeared to her that the arm was somehow stuck. As the child manipulated the limb, it suddenly broke off without any warning. The child turned to his mother, holding up the broken piece, with a saddened expression on his face.

"Look, mother," he said. "It's broken. Can you fix it?" The mother took the piece lovingly.

"I will take it to the carpenter," she said. "He can fix it for you, son."

"Yes, mother," the boy said.

They talked and laughed about it in the pleasant afternoon shade of the trees. The women smiled cordially at each other in the refreshing breeze as they witnessed the child's play. They were oblivious to the tiny, ugly black worm that crawled out of the broken arm. It squirmed along the wood, the movement catching the mother's attention. When she saw the revolting creature, she reacted as though she had seen the worst horror in her life. She stared at it with an expression of fear that alarmed Madeleine.

"Agh!" the mother screamed, reacting reflexively to the worm's grotesque appearance. She threw the wood to the ground in disgust, turned to Madeleine, who was watching the whole event, and said, "What IS that?" pointing to the unfamiliar organism.

Madeleine stared at the wood fragment as well, unable to identify the worm poking out of the wood's orifice. Curiosity compelled her to pick it up, however. That's when she saw a second worm emerge. She, too, reacted by instinctively dropping the wood as though it were plagued with a dreadful disease. The women studied the two black worms with orange rings around their bellies that had crawled out of the wood.

The boy's mother stepped on the worms instinctively, and turned to Madeleine, picking up the pieces to hand to her. Madeleine shook her head as she accepted them.

"I will take these pieces and the dead worms to the carpenter," Madeleine said. "He will know what to do. I will tell you what he says when he examines it."

She left the park, walking straight back to Gilbert's shop. Along the way, several people stopped her to say that they also had found little black worms in their children's wooden toys. One woman even threatened the carpenter and yelled, "He's a cheat!" Madeleine experienced a fear unlike that which she knew from the landlord. It was a fear of unknown forces. Where had these worms come from and why?

Swinging the big stable door open, Madeleine ran inside, where she found Gilbert busy at work. He came to greet her when he heard her approach.

"What is it, Madeleine?" he said.

She clutched his hand, forcing him back into his shop, where there was good light from his lamp. She pulled the pieces from her dress pocket. He stared at them for a long time. He picked up one of the pieces to examine.

"What is it, Gilbert?" Madeleine wondered.

"These are borer beetle larvae," he said, instantly recognizing them. "Where did you get this?"

"It's a piece of one of the toys you made." Gilbert scratched his head.

"How'd larvae get into this wood? There were none in the trees from which I took the wood."

"I have never seen these in Auguliere, ever," Madeleine assured. He pried open the piece of the aspen to find a hollow with a tiny white sphere.

"These are eggs," Gilbert said.

"There is an infestation?" Madeleine said, alarmed.

Gilbert ran to his storage room to pull out a box of toys made with the aspen. It was crawling with black worms. When Madeleine caught up to him, she put her hand to her mouth and gasped when she saw the infestation.

Oleg heard the commotion and came out of her room. She must have been asleep because her face was creased from her pillow. She forced open her eyes, surprised to see Madeleine.

"What's going on here?" she said sleepily.

"I need to see what's happening in the parks," Gilbert said.

"The trees!" Madeleine said. "Oh, no!"

Gilbert nodded affirmatively, reaching for his horses. He hitched them up and led them out of the stable. Outside, he helped Madeleine climb onto the wagon. He drove the team past the market, up to the park. It was still light enough to see the damage to the aspen trees. When Gilbert and Madeleine arrived at the park, he jumped from the wagon, helping Madeleine by offering his hand. They quickly scampered up the little incline on the path to the grove of aspen trees.

"Let's not arouse suspicion that anything is wrong," Madeleine said. They stepped off the walkways, between the shrubs and trees. Gilbert began to examine the bark. He shook his head in disgust.

"What is it?" Madeleine asked, worriedly.

"Just as I suspected," Gilbert said. "They're all infested with these black worms just like the aspen wood in the shop."

"That's awful, Gil," Madeleine said. "Do you think it's all over town? What are we to do?"

"We'll check on a few places where I did work," Gilbert said. "Let's see if they are affected."

They both climbed back in the wagon and drove out to the Winthrop farm. They arrived just in time to see Mr. Winthrop burning the wood. He shook his fist at the carpenter as he approached.

"What's happened?" Gilbert yelled.

"You know quite well, sir," Mr. Winthrop said.

"I see you're taking a wise precaution."

"Wise, indeed!" Mr. Winthrop said. "Wise not to engage the likes of your services again." Madeleine turned to Gilbert, frightened.

"It looks like the whole town's falling apart," Madeleine said. "Let's get the wagon back to the stable."

"Yes," Gilbert said. "That's probably a wise idea."

They drove the wagon past the market and town center. There were people standing by the big well. When the wagon came by, a chicken farmer noticed him.

"There he is!" the chicken farmer said, shaking his fist at the wagon as it rolled by.

"The Knesnovich girl's involved in a conspiracy!" yelled a farm hand.

"He cheated us," shouted another.

Madeleine searched Gilbert's face as the wagon bounced along. She tried to feel positive about his work, but she felt her confidence slipping away each time another individual pointed a finger at Gilbert. It made her feel sick to her stomach. She sought out his face and stared into his eyes, causing him to turn toward her as he drove.

"Your work's not really inferior, Gilbert, is it?" Gilbert regarded Madeleine without answering, as though he were ashamed.

"Of course not!" he said, as though he had to defend himself.

"How could this happen?"

The self-doubt still would not leave his mind. After a brief time, Gilbert faced Madeleine with renewed awareness.

"Nothing natural I know could cause an infestation as suddenly as this." Madeleine looked strangely at Gilbert the way a dog wonders what his master is thinking.

"Are you saying the infestation is not natural?"

"That is what I am saying," Gilbert said. Madeleine could sense the relief in Gilbert's tone.

"Could the landlord stoop that low?" Madeleine whispered to herself, but loud enough for Gilbert to hear.

"I hate to think any man would be so destructive."

"You don't know Mr. Robertson," Madeleine said.

"That's what Vladimir told me," Gilbert said. "I have seen him in action."

"His actions speak very loud."

"There is no man beyond salvation." Madeleine looked up at Gilbert, pursing her lips in an artificial smile.

The wagon bounced along the road. Occasionally, when someone saw it drive by, he or she pointed to the wagon and jeered at the carpenter. Word seemed to have gotten out so that even those who didn't know him recognized the wagon when it drove by.

Women came out of their shanties to stand on the cobblestone streets when the wagon drove past. They shouted loudly.

"You'd better watch out for that carpenter," said an old woman.

"His work is inferior and his wood is riddled with worms," another yelled.

When the wagon finally turned onto the dirt street where the stable was, four women came out onto the street.

"That carpenter is cheap," the first one said.

"He builds his products poorly," said another.

"They fall apart," said a young woman. She turned toward the others.

"You see, he's a heartbreaker."

"We can't stand for this. We have to tell Mr. Robertson."

"He'll do something about this carpenter," the oldest said.

Gilbert drove the wagon back into the stable. Madeleine said good night as soon as she got down from the carriage. She returned to the safety of her shanty. Gilbert tended his horses then climbed into his bed in the wagon. He wondered about the landlord. From the deepest regions of his mind, Mrs. Teivel came into his conscience.

Meanwhile, the landlord waited on the edge of town with his wagon pulled by a team of mules. He watched with satisfaction as the townspeople struggled with the new plague. People started running to neighbors, discussing the problems and taking up the issue. Gilbert didn't know the townspeople were starting to turn against him. Several people ran by the landlord's wagon shouting, "That carpenter is deceptive. His products fall apart."

"His work is inferior, Mr. Robertson," one of them said, approaching the wagon.

"What're you gonna do about him?" said another.

The landlord surveyed the gathering of townspeople and stroked his beard. The mules stood almost motionless in their position, hitched to the wagon. He drew his head up and smiled to himself with malevolent satisfaction.

Chapter 17

Gilbert rose early the next morning, eager to repair some toys that were brought to his attention. While he was absorbed in his work, a loud crash disturbed the tranquility of his shop. He looked about him but was unable to determine what had caused it. Perhaps men were loading wood in a wagon or something was being unloaded in the street. Maybe he could inquire about it after lunch. Twenty minutes later, he heard sounds of scuffling and running in the street. He peeked out of his window, but nothing stirred. After a few more minutes, Madeleine disturbed the silence when she burst into the stable. Her hair was unkempt and flecked with dust. Her face glowed red with tears streaming down her cheeks. Somehow, he didn't connect Madeleine to the awful crash, yet he saw the urgency in her contorted face once she came close.

"Gilbert!" she shouted, approaching the shop door. He set the toy parts down on the workbench thoughtfully. "He did it again!" Gilbert stepped away from the bench as Madeleine raced toward him, bearing an agonized expression.

"I don't know what I'm going to do," she screamed, straining her neck muscles, thrashing her hands as she continued screaming. As Gilbert attempted to calm her down, her frantic words were reduced to rambling.

"Slow down," Gilbert said. "I can't understand a word you're saying." He confronted her, grabbing her shoulders. "Sit down and tell me about it." He took out his big red handkerchief and wiped her tear-drenched face. "Start at the beginning."

"It's the landlord," she said, reaching up to her wet cheeks. "He smashed Oleg's stable, destroyed all the wooden baskets and tools you made and ruined the entire cache of toys of all the children in Auguliere."

"Oh, no!" Gilbert said, clasping his hands together. "He has to be stopped."

Madeleine saw the deep concern displayed on Gilbert's face as he agonized over what she told him.

"Calm down now," Gilbert said, holding her shoulders. "We'll find a way."

"Why is he such an evil man?" she sobbed, burying her head in his shoulder.

"Don't worry," Gilbert assured her. "Good always triumphs over evil." She glared at his eyes, her lips firm. In her thoughts, she challenged what she had learned about good and evil as a child.

"Does it?" Madeleine said, looking straight at his face. Gilbert led her into his storage room as he listened to her. "It's easy for you to say."

"We'll work together," Gilbert said, turning back to her.

"You always have such a positive attitude," Madeleine said. "This time he's gone too far. There's no hope. What am I going to do, Gilbert? What am I going to do?"

"We'll think of something."

"He'll tear my shanty down like he did Pavel's."

"I could sell one of my horses," Gilbert promised.

"I couldn't let you do that."

"I have another," he assured.

"No," Madeleine said. "That's a foolish choice. You need your horses."

"Why don't you sell the medallion so you can pay your bills?"

"Oh, no! I couldn't do that," Madeleine said. "That medal represents all of my father's hard work. I am proud of it. I shall never sell it, even if I am starving." She surprised him by her directness.

"I guess you're right," Gilbert said, pulling out racks to examine them. "If I had been blessed with one, I wouldn't sell it either." Madeleine looked at him strangely, wondering if he meant something else.

"There must be a better way."

"Come with me to the town center," Gilbert insisted. "I have to see if what I am thinking is true."

"What are you thinking?" Madeleine said. "Is there something wrong?"

"There may be and I have to find out if some things I know about Auguliere are true."

"You can be really mysterious when you want to be," Madeleine said.

"I don't mean to be."

Gilbert's uncharacteristic behavior troubled Madeleine. She felt trapped in her thoughts, unable to find the key to Gilbert's motives. It seemed to Madeleine the window into Gilbert's mind was closing with the passage of time, making her feel even more bewildered.

They walked to the well where Gilbert observed men chopping some infested aspen boards. Across the street a mule team waited to cart off more wood. Others then gathered, some with carts and ponies.

Madeleine tried to see the whole development from Gilbert's eyes. She understood he could do no wrong in her mind. Even though she trusted him implicitly, she knew the infestation was beyond him. She looked up to him with her wide, receptive smile and attempted to understand the situation.

"Oh, Gilbert," Madeleine said, at his side. "It seems like everything we've worked for is falling apart." Gilbert remained focused on the horses. "First my father's barn, then Oleg's shanty, and now this awful infestation."

Gilbert looked over the horse's mane and stared at Mrs. Teivel's shop. Madeleine realized Gilbert had discovered something that bothered him, but she had to endure an agonizing waiting period until he felt ready to talk about it.

As if seized by a curse, his expression changed from innocence to petulance. He halted the animals and stared at the shop.

"Now I see the connection," Gilbert said.

"To the wood?" Madeleine asked.

"To the landlord," Gilbert said. Madeleine remained puzzled, casting her head down. "Now I understand why her shop is brick . . ."

When she glanced up again, this time at Mrs. Teivel's shop, she saw Greta pass by. She seemed to be looking for something. Even though Madeleine wanted to call to her, she refrained, in deference to Gilbert's discovery.

"I promise you, Madeleine," Gilbert said. "I will find a cure for the beetles."

"I hope so," she said, fearful. "Gilbert, I am so scared." She clutched his arm, pressing close to him. "I don't understand what is going on. I know if the landlord does something, he'll do it under cover of darkness so that he's not found out." Madeleine's eyes were still puffy and red.

"We'll find a way to overcome this," Gilbert assured. "I'm going to talk to Vladimir. He has authority."

"It's so hopeless. It feels like this is the end of my young life. I cannot overcome this." She looked up at him for his strong support, but she didn't feel it this time. She shivered instead.

"Oh, Gilbert!" she cried in despair. "What will I do? What will I do? What will I do?" Gilbert couldn't respond, as if a terrible thought prevented him.

Chapter 18

A rooster's crow awakened Madeleine in the predawn fog. She coughed and cleared her throat in the damp air before she rose to sit at her tiny vanity. She gazed into the mirror and thought to herself, "I am getting old! Yet I am still a maiden in Auguliere." She turned her face to examine each side. "Let's face it, Madeleine, you're going to be an old maid." She let the ends of her lips point down in a frown.

Iakov still slept, even though Madeleine rattled the kettle on her grate. She piled the hearth with kindling and struck a match to ignite the pile. The fire flared and gave off its welcomed instant warmth. Madeleine imagined various ways she could settle her debt, watching the majestic dance of the flames. Her sisters only briefly came to mind, making Madeleine wonder what her father had meant from previous discussions, when he indicated they would help. She turned around when she saw her father struggling to navigate the doorway with his bulky chair.

"Father, you are up early," she said, combing her hair back with her fingers. Iakov's admiration for her made her conscious of her sisters' relationship with their father.

"I was bothered by the troubled expression on your face," he said.

"Father," Madeleine said, not realizing that her troubled face betrayed her. She speculated how her father could sense her worry. "How did you see that?"

"I saw the look on your face last night before we retired," Iakov said, convincingly. "I know what is going on. You try to shield me, child. I have already lived your life more than three times."

"Yes, father," Madeleine said. "You have told me many times."

"So, what is the news you have?"

"No news, father."

"Oh," Iakov said. "I will have to whittle it out of the carpenter?"

"You don't have to whittle it out of anyone," Madeleine assured. "There is nothing hidden from you."

"No, only denied," Iakov insisted, repositioning himself.

"Father!" Madeleine rose and strode to his chair.

"I see. I must be content to be an old man." This saddened Madeleine.

"Father." She pulled the wheelchair over the doorway's threshold.

"You will find a source of revenue from your siblings," He wheeled up to the table where he expected his morning tea.

"Really, father!" Madeleine said. "Revenue?" Again, she recalled numerous times he mentioned them.

"Why do you always doubt me?"

"I am not doubting you. It's just that I know how they are."

"How are they?" When the whistle blew, she retrieved the kettle, placed it on the table in front of her father, and filled his cup.

"I . . . I," she hesitated.

"You really don't know because you haven't visited them in years."

"I wonder why?" Madeleine sat next to him.

"Yes, I do indeed wonder why."

The knock at the door disturbed their chat, and brought Madeleine again to her feet. She thought she saw the hinges shake when the visitor pounded on the door again. Each step she took toward it made her hesitate before the next. *Who would be calling on her at this hour*, she thought. When she finally opened it, she found the most fragrant and rich bouquet waiting for her in the carpenter's hands. This brought a wonderful, warm reaction to Madeleine's face and made her completely forget her father's disagreement.

"You're up so early," Madeleine said.

She stood on tiptoe to compete with Gilbert's height, in a receptive gesture, but Gilbert stood stiff, careful to avoid eye contact when he bowed his head in the doorway, offering the blooms. She accepted the flowers from him, sniffing their fragrance as she walked through the rooms in search for a vase.

"I am up with my horses," he said.

He did bring some of the familiar horse odor with him, although Madeleine had gotten used to it and didn't at all mind. He dipped below the jamb and entered. She led him into the kitchen, where she found a clay pitcher.

"I was making tea for father. Would you like some?"

"That is very kind of you," Gilbert said. "I can never turn down the wholesome flavor of your tea."

"I will also bake biscuits in the hearth," Madeleine added.

"Much obliged, ma'am."

Gilbert sat at the familiar table, between Iakov's wheelchair and Madeleine's seat. He watched Madeleine prepare all the morning commodities. Iakov sat quietly in his chair and took the hot cup to his quivering lips.

"And you, sir," Gilbert said. "How are you feelin' on such a fine day in the valley?"

"Fine day, indeed!" Iakov said. "I have heard of the blight affecting your wood."

Gilbert bowed his head in anguish, not knowing what to say. Madeleine noticed Gilbert's sad expression. She looked at her father, hoping he could cheer him up.

"I am ever so sorry," Gilbert said.

"There's no need to apologize to me. Can't you see some just aren't content to see folks happy?" Iakov said.

"Some people have priorities," Gilbert said.

"Indeed, son. Priorities!"

"Father," Madeleine said, wiping the slurped tea from his lips. "Why are you so argumentative today?"

Iakov stopped talking when Madeleine served the hot tea to the carpenter. He appeared more worried, even though he sat with a reservation on his face that baffled Madeleine.

"I may have a way to fight the blight," Gilbert suddenly said, surprising Madeleine and Iakov. Iakov raised his eyebrows, making him appear more alert. Gilbert took notice, sipping the hot tea. Madeleine sat down, placing the hot biscuits on the table. The men grabbed the fresh morsels, eager to sample their goodness.

"We had insect infestations," Iakov said, munching chewy grains. "We used the sap of the pine trees to kill them." Gilbert stroked his beardless chin and smiled.

"We are dealing with a much more aggressive creature." Gilbert glanced at the hearth and sniffed the fresh biscuits, waiting patiently for the next batch while Iakov waited for Gilbert to continue. "It calls for a much more aggressive remedy." Iakov was somehow ready for Gilbert's tone.

"My father taught me well about the nature of the Earth's bounty. He taught me every creature of the earth, including man, has an enemy." Iakov raised his eyebrows again.

"What enemy do these pernicious insects have?" Iakov said.

"There is a tiny creature that lives in the ground," Gilbert said, stuffing his mouth with a biscuit.

"So there are many tiny creatures that live in the ground."

"Not like this one," Gilbert said, trying to swallow. "He has a special gift."

"What kind of gift is so special?" Iakov said.

"You need a glass to see him." Madeleine kept quiet while the men spoke.

"You need a glass to see many creatures," Iakov insisted.

"These creatures eat the grubs of the beetle." Now Iakov pulled up closer to the table, far more interested than before. "His name is *nematode*."

"I never heard of such a creature," Iakov said. "It almost sounds mythical."

"It is not a fictional creature," Gilbert assured. "These creatures are quite real."

"Where do we find them?" Iakov cleared his throat from the raspy grain.

"They can be found anywhere, but they must be delivered in large numbers to be effective."

"Where can we find them in large numbers?"

"We cannot," Gilbert said. Iakov scratched his scrawny gray beard while they both became serious. Madeleine laughed.

"First you say we must find them in large numbers," Madeleine said. "Then you say we cannot."

Gilbert carefully examined Madeleine's naïve expression, regarding her with laughter.

"We must culture them, Madeleine."

"Culture them?" Iakov said. Turning to Madeleine he nodded affirmatively, "He means farm them."

"Yes," Gilbert said. "Your father is quite right. It is based on a farming technique."

"How will you do that?" Madeleine added.

"I have a plan," Gilbert said.

Madeleine sat closer to her father, and both listened to Gilbert like children ready for a bedtime story. Iakov's ears even perked up, making Madeleine feel protected.

"I will take the boy with me on my wagon up in the meadows. We shall take the soil samples from various locations. They prefer to live in certain places. We will eventually find them."

"What if you don't find any?" Madeleine speculated.

"You have to be positive, Madeleine," Iakov said.

"Oh," Gilbert said, wearing a stilted smile, "we will find them. When we do, I shall take them back to the shop where I will cultivate them."

"You mean feed them!" Iakov chuckled.

"Indeed," Gilbert assured, taking his cup to his lips. "They will be fed."

"They will be fat!" Iakov said, laughing.

"You are a genius," Madeleine said, tilting her head as she smiled affectionately.

"I am just a man with some knowledge."

"Aye," Iakov said, "and a wise one."

That afternoon, Gilbert took Pavel with him to the meadows in search of nematodes. They rode the trail out to the meadows on the east end where the grass becomes high along the creek bed. They stopped the wagon there. Gilbert slid the shovel into the soft dirt, pushing it deep into the earth with his boot. Pavel peered into the shovel of dirt to see what it contained, and immediately withdrew and gasped.

"What's the matter, Pavel?" Gilbert said.

The boy pointed, terrified. Gilbert reached into the dirt, pulled out one of the wriggling creatures and laughed.

"It's an earthworm."

Pavel was still afraid of them until Gilbert placed one in his hand and showed it to the boy, assuring him it wouldn't bite or hurt him. Pavel smiled and poked at it with his finger apprehensively. Gilbert allowed the boy to explore this new creature so he could feel comfortable among the creatures of the earth.

"They won't hurt you, Pavel. These are nature's dirt cleaners," Gilbert said. "They only eat dead plants." Pavel pointed excitedly.

"Earthworm!" Pavel said, spreading a joyous smile on his little face. He jumped up and down shouting, "Earthworm, earthworm!"

"Yes, my little friend," Gilbert said. "Earthworm. Now you've learned a new word."

They took samples of soil from different places. After many trials, Gilbert found a nematode. He waved his hand and yelled, "Pavel!" Pavel immediately ran to him. When he came near, Gilbert showed him the setup. "Look through the glass, Pavel and you'll see them." Pavel knelt in the dirt and squinted into the glass. For a moment, he was still. He suddenly jumped back.

"Gil, Gil!" he screamed. "I see tode. I see!"

His excitement was explosive. The joy he experienced radiated with lasting effects. The boy was so happy the moment made Gilbert also cry with glee. He watched the boy with pride as he observed this new microscopic world. It reminded him of his own childhood, when he discovered metal and wood to which his father introduced him.

"Yes," Gilbert said, "we found them."

"Nematode!" Pavel said, filled with mirth. It was as though Pavel added a new dimension to his life, savoring the ripple effects of his elation.

As the day ended, the tired nematode scouts took the wagon down the valley back to their shop. Madeleine watched them through the window as they worked late into the night. She watched them stacking crates into the shelves on the wall of the shop. She only saw dirt in each crate. Tool-clanking sounds pierced the still night air. This made her feel happy, but somehow afraid. When she returned to her room, she couldn't help wonder what was becoming of Auguliere. Could Gilbert really find a cure for this atrocious infestation or was he just kidding everybody? Many times, she found malevolent expressions on people's faces whenever she heard them speak of the carpenter.

"His craftsmanship is failing," one remarked

"He doesn't know the wood," another speculated.

"He's taking us for granted," still another assumed.

The next day Madeleine saw that the boys were up early, organizing and building their shop's equipment. The shop acquired a new appearance. The heavy tools Gilbert had used to cut wood were now pushed aside, to make way for shelves filled with small crates with dirt samples that contained nematodes. She resisted the temptation to visit the shop and stayed with her father. She feared Gilbert would resent her meddling in his project. She had to be content to let Gilbert succeed. Her father made her understand Gilbert's work was necessary to save Auguliere. When Madeleine came into the kitchen, she found her father already looking through the window.

"He is such an industrious person, child."

"Yes, father. He is. Why is there such despair that our wonderful village has come to this? Only the people on the very edge of the village have not felt the effects of the beetles."

"Oh, they will. They like the softwood, like pine and aspen. All the maple and birch are relatively safe."

"So, Gilbert's shop is safe?"

"I believe it is, child."

By the third day, the shop looked more like a laboratory than before. Madeleine still limited her observation to a window view. She also knew they were too busy to fix food. She found it necessary to prepare a basket and pay them a little visit.

"Pavel," Gilbert called. "Hand me that tray." The boy handed the tray to Gilbert and looked up to him ready for his next command.

"We shall take the grubs and introduce them to the culture." Pavel watched, fascinated.

"Look at them under the glass."

"Ah!" Pavel exclaimed, amazed. "Tode." He pointed. "Many todes."

"Yes, Pavel," Gilbert confirmed. "They are eating the grubs. We need to keep feeding the nematodes to culture them. When we have millions of them, we shall be ready."

"Mil?" Pavel said.

"Millions." Gilbert confirmed again.

Gilbert looked up from his work when Pavel sat on the table to watch him. He gestured. Pavel turned around. The boy smiled.

"Madeleine," he said.

"He said my name!" Madeleine remarked.

"Yes," Gilbert said, smiling proudly.

"He never did that before."

"The more he hangs around you," Madeleine said, "the better he seems to speak."

"I know," Gilbert said. "How's your situation?"

"Here," she said, handing him the basket.

"You didn't have to do that," Gilbert said.

"I don't like to do things I have to do," Madeleine said.

"Thanks," Gilbert said.

The hungry boys devoured the food. Madeleine watched them eat. She returned to her shanty to tend to her chores. Gilbert continued to work throughout the day.

When Madeleine went to the market, she had to shun people there who made negative comments about the carpenter. She refused to hear them.

That night when Madeleine returned home, she saw his lamp. She sprang from her window to visit the laboratory. It made her recall the olden days when her father conducted experiments. Like her father, Gilbert meticulously organized his trays and arranged his tools. Madeleine took in a deep breath as she watched with admiration as he worked. The boy also helped to complete the picture, making her feel even more drawn in, reflecting on the brother she never had.

It took a while before Gilbert seemed to notice her. He was too preoccupied with his mission. He sent the boy back and forth to shelves, pulling them out and placing new ones in empty racks.

"You will be among the first to know the nematode family is growing," Gilbert told Madeleine. She regarded Oleg peeking at the carpenter's activities from her door.

"So is your stable family," Madeleine smirked.

"Once we have the insect problem under control, we can forge ahead," Gilbert said.

"No," Madeleine said, "you can forge ahead. I'm stuck in a rut. From my point of view, it looks like everyone's against me. I know it's just a matter of time."

"Let's try to reason out the problem," Gilbert said.

"The trouble is you're always 'reasoning out the problem.' You never look at yourself." Gilbert showed a shameful look on his face.

"You're right," Gilbert said. "I am not sensitive enough to your needs." Madeleine was nearly crying.

"I'm sorry, Gilbert," Madeleine admitted. "I know you really mean well."

"Look," Gilbert said. "The landlord wants his money. He's figured out a way to take away all of your income. He destroyed your farm with water restrictions. He foreclosed on your father's stable. What about your chickens and eggs?"

"It's not enough," Madeleine said. "He'll find a way to destroy them, too."

"Don't you have any other relatives?"

"My mother died when I was young."

"No siblings?"

"I have sisters on the North Slope."

"Have they come to visit you and your father?"

"No, they don't come."

"Have you visited them?"

"On occasion."

"The last occasion?"

"Years."

"Why not visit them?"

"They are stingy and would not help."

"Why not just visit them. You never know the good there is in a person until you explore it."

"What you say may have truth, at least the way you said it."

"You won't know until you try it."

"I may just do that."

"Good," Gilbert said. "You will make them happy. Perhaps they will think about seeing their father."

"Perhaps."

"You never know."

Madeleine left the shop, daydreaming all the way home.

Chapter 19

Madeleine felt comfortable in the morning. The birds sang, occasionally some dogs barked; otherwise, the village was quiet. She rested on the edge of her bed while visions of her sisters entered her mind. She remembered with joy the fun they had when her mother was still alive and all five were a family. They lived in the last house of the cobblestone road on the north side of town where the hill began to slope up. Each morning her father drove their wagon through the center of town, past the markets and big well, to his workshop. In those days, all the buildings were new. The floors were tight and didn't squeak and birds flew in from all over the valley just to see how beautiful Auguliere really was. They picked at the straw on the vendors' carts to build their nests in the aspen trees in the parks. After Mrs. Knesnovich died, Iakov bought the shanty adjacent to the stable so he didn't have far to travel to his shop. He let his two older daughters live in the house because they never indicated an interest in marriage.

It was different now, Madeleine mused as she took her pony and wagon to visit her sisters. The heavy timbers, which once adorned the architecture, were gray and splintered. Years of wear were etched in the surface. Spaces opened where the wood came together. Many pieces failed altogether and some houses were condemned as unsafe.

Madeleine made the pony halt. She climbed out of the wagon and hitched the animal to the post. She patted his head lovingly as she walked away and headed toward the dilapidated shanty. She picked up the giant zinc knocker and allowed it to drop, sending a loud metallic clinking announcing her presence. The big wooden door swung open. Both of the women inside gaped at their younger sister in surprise. Penelope was the older of the two.

"Madeleine," Penelope said. "What are you doing here?"

"Just visiting," Madeleine said. She stood at the door waiting to be invited in.

"Did you put on some weight, Madeleine?" Marjorie asked, standing behind Penelope.

"Yes," Penelope chided, in agreement, "she does fill out her dress." Marjorie nodded. Madeleine regarded the women with a blank expression, expecting them to fling other insults at her. She let her head lean to one side with a smile.

"Good afternoon, Marjorie; good afternoon, Penelope," Madeleine said in a soft, sweet tone, still standing outside. The two sisters stood like a blockade at the door, making Madeleine feel as though she must wait until they were ready to let her pass. Madeleine shifted her weight from one foot to the other, patiently waiting to be invited in.

"Do you expect me to believe you came clear 'cross town just to see us?" Marjorie said, looking at Penelope in disbelief and tightening her thin lips.

"I brought you some things," Madeleine said, lifting the basket for both sisters to see. After what seemed like an eternity, they finally led her into the house. Madeleine stopped by the table to place her basket on top. The two sisters eagerly helped unload the tomatoes and eggs.

"I see your coops are intact," Marjorie said, combing her fingers through her hair as she waltzed into the next room to find an easy chair.

"Are you still managing father's shop?" Penelope asked, plopping herself on a chair near Marjorie.

"I found a tenant for the shop," Madeleine said, stepping into the den where the sisters sat.

"Really?" Penelope said, crossing her legs. "I would have thought it collapsed by now."

"Gilbert's repairing it."

"Gilbert, is it?" Marjorie said. She leaned forward, resting her elbows on her knees.

"Father's sitting by idly as usual?" said Penelope, still sitting straight.

"Father has gotten worse. Gilbert is very helpful."

"Is he?" Marjorie said, letting her face show interest.

"I'll bet," said Penelope, grinning. Madeleine shrugged her shoulders.

"Give Madeleine a chance, Penelope."

"I was recalling the days when mother was alive," Madeleine said, looking up at the ceiling dreamy-eyed. She evened out her dress's collar while she searched for a job for her other hand.

"Oh, yes," Penelope said, adjusting the belt that bound her dress, letting her heavy breasts dance with her movement, catching Madeleine's attention. "Indeed, she was a darling,"

"She had such a dramatic way," Marjorie continued. "Do you remember our little amphitheatre?" Madeleine looked away, pinching her lips tightly together, reflecting on the old days when she was carefree.

"We children used to crawl under the stage when the actors were playing roles," Madeleine said, tossing her locks back. Madeleine looked at each sister for a time, waiting for a response. Madeleine soon learned responses from her sisters were slow to come.

"Oh, yes. Who used to hide in the water closet?" Marjorie said, making Madeleine blush.

"You and Greta played a game there, by the stables," Penelope reminded her.

"That's not all you did by the stables . . ." Marjorie insisted. The sisters checked each other's smiles and giggled.

"The other girl and Vladimir," Penelope said.

"Vladimir? I would never!" Madeleine said, trying to look proper. The three giggled, remembering old times.

"All that's gone now," Marjorie said, changing to a serious tone. "Except for Aunt Emma."

Madeleine gawked at the girls strangely, trying to recall the familiar name. Madeleine observed that her sisters had a much clearer recollection of these events.

"It's the old stable lady," Penelope clarified.

"Oh," Madeleine said. "She must be old."

"She's still rich," Marjorie said.

"She needs help," Penelope said.

"Like father?"

"Only she has money," Penelope said.

"Money?" Madeleine enquired, "Hm!"

"Money to pay for a companion," Penelope said.

"Oh yeah?" Madeleine said, surprised, turning to Penelope with renewed interest.

"We are not able to do it," Marjorie confirmed, moving a little forward.

"Perhaps you know someone who could take care of her?" Penelope asked.

"As a matter of fact, I do."

"Anyone we know?" Marjorie said, lifting her elbows.

"As a matter of fact, yes." Again, Madeleine adjusted herself. Madeleine remembered how one sister would always set up the other to boast about something. This time Madeleine wanted to take center stage.

"Who?" Penelope proposed.

"Me!" Madeleine suggested with finality.

"You?" Marjorie asked, surprised. "What about your farm and father's shop?"

"The landlord foreclosed and now collects the rent, the drought has killed the last of our corn and most of the other products are gone. I have the time."

"Father?" Penelope asked.

"He sleeps most of the day."

"Maybe you should see her," Marjorie speculated.

The chat diminished as noon arrived. Madeleine took notice neither sister made an effort to offer any lunch, not even from the basket she brought. Not even tea! After two hours passed, Madeleine was motivated to leave. Anyway, she needed to go find Emma.

In the afternoon, Madeleine climbed into her buggy and had her pony pull the rig along the bumpy road until they arrived at the old woman's house. It wasn't like her sister's. It was huge with two levels and an attic, plus a root cellar where she stored her tools.

Madeleine stopped her animal, hitched him to the post and climbed up the wooden steps, out of the muddy street. The big zinc knocker bore Emma's name, inscribed in the metal. She yelled, "Push it and enter." Madeleine pushed the huge door, letting it pivot on its creaking hinges. Madeleine looked inside the quiet house, recalling its special smell. It looked exactly as she remembered it, with knick-knacks strewn all over, covering every table, every stand and in every corner, making the place look like a museum. When she walked into the parlor, Madeleine saw the old woman. She had aged. She was no longer the nimble old lady who barked commands and directed people. She had languished in the gloom of her self-made prison. Now she was an invalid. She picked her hand up lazily and said, "Young lady, do I know you?"

"Aunt Emma, it's me, Madeleine."

"Madeleine?" Aunt Emma said. "I don't know any Madeleine."

"It's Madeleine, the 'elf.' Remember when I used to climb on the stalls of the ponies?"

"Madeleine?" she said. "Madeleine!"

"Yes."

"Madeleine," she thought. "That Madeleine!"

"We used to play as children."

"Yes, now I remember," Aunt Emma said. "You grew up."

"You've changed, too."

"Yes. I became old. I can't walk anymore and I can't take care of my ponies. I am what you call *retired*."

"Penelope and Marjorie were telling me. They told me you needed help."

"Yes, I do. Do you know anyone who could do it?"

"Yes, me."

"You! But . . . but," she babbled, helplessly.

"Aunt Emma, I need the money. My father's ill, my crops have failed, my chickens are dying and Mr. Robertson foreclosed on my father's stables."

"Child!"

"Please! I know so much about those animals."

"Well, it never occurred to me the daughter of Iakov Knesnovich would ever need a hand. Then, we are all human beings, capable of frailty."

"Well, we need one, Aunt Emma." The old woman shifted, mumbled softly, avoiding eye contact with Madeleine. She turned her head without losing sense of where Madeleine was.

"I suppose I could let you do it. This place needs a lot of work. I have a million errands. I can only give you a wage of fifty rubles a month."

"That's more than enough. When can I start?"

"Start tomorrow morning."

"I will be up with the roosters," Madeleine said.

"Just like Iakov," Emma remarked, puffing up her chubby cheeks. Madeleine left in good spirits, although she felt sorry leaving Aunt Emma, who waved good-bye in the gloomy old house.

Madeleine smiled to herself happily as she marched off, singing, "A workday's ahead for Madeleine. A duty's callin' her now . . . A workday's saved Madeleine from drudging behind a plow . . . A workday's saved Knesnovich's house, Emma's plight is solved, along with Madeleine's troubles. Now I'm glad I got involved. I'm a working woman, with too many chores to do. I'm a working woman, with so many things to renew . . ." Madeleine was truly uplifted. Her spirit followed her all the way to her pony, even through the mud. She untied the animal and climbed on her wagon, letting him pull her along the dirt road.

"I can't wait to see the look in Gilbert's eyes," she thought.

For the first time in months, she felt rejuvenated. She shook the reins, "Ck, ck," and whistled to her pony as the animal pulled the wagon along. It would still be several hours before Madeleine returned home. She made it a point to stop and tell everyone she knew along the way. She amused herself by singing her newly composed song as she rode.

Chapter 20

That same afternoon, Pavel and Gilbert were playing with a game Gilbert had made. When Gilbert said he would leave to see Madeleine, Pavel immediately wanted to come along. The boy grabbed hold of Gilbert's trousers and wouldn't let them go.

"Pavel, you just stay here and play in the shop. I am just going to see Madeleine." The boy's head drooped sadly, almost letting his hair touch the dirt floor. He wore a frown that disturbed Gilbert. "When I come back, I'm going to show you what we'll do next in the shop."

"I want to go see Madeleine." He smiled to himself, holding his arms up. "I love Madeleine."

"So do I," Gilbert said, adjusting himself to the realization of what he said. "Come along, Pavel. You can wait in her garden."

"I wait, Gil. I wait," Pavel said as they walked to the rear of Madeleine's shanty.

"The time has come for Madeleine to see our work. I want it to be set up right. That's why I have to do it this way."

"I wait. I will," Pavel assured Gilbert.

When Gilbert and Pavel arrived at Madeleine's shanty, he instructed the boy to play in the garden. He lifted the big zinc knocker and let it go, making the whole door vibrate.

He waited patiently for the familiar scuffling sound, but it was quiet. He listened for the faint sounds of life inside, but none stirred. Madeleine was not home.

"I'll be back later," Gilbert said to Pavel. "You can stay here and play." Pavel smiled and continued to play, accepting his assignment. "When Madeleine returns, Pavel, let me know."

"Ya, ya," Pavel answered, looking back at Gilbert, showing he understood. Gilbert smiled. "Ya, Gil." Gilbert returned to the shop.

Later that afternoon, Gilbert returned to Madeleine's shanty, finding Pavel right where he had left him in the garden playing with his toys. He looked up at Gilbert.

"Hey, big guy," Gilbert said. "Did she come home?"

"No, Gil. She not here."

"I'm going to leave her a note, Pavel."

He pushed the door to find it swung open. He walked into the shanty quietly. He looked around, gently calling Madeleine's name. She did not answer. He concluded she was still not there. He had looked into her empty bedroom, pulling at his chin with one hand, wondering where she could be. When he moved to the other room, he saw her father sleeping. He backed out of the room so as not to disturb him.

Then in the common kitchen, he observed the ingot in its place on the mantel. He advanced towards it. He picked it up, examined it and said to himself, "This is just what I was looking for. I don't think Madeleine will mind. Maybe I should leave her a note. I shall write it on this parchment I carry and use my quill."

He departed feeling proud, knowing he intended to do something to benefit Madeleine and her father. Pavel remained, playing in the garden, and giggled, "Gil, Gil." Gilbert winked as he walked off.

Chapter 21

Two hours later, the landlord came snooping around the shanty. Dogs began to bark when he stepped onto the property, but they failed to stop him. He hesitated before he let the big knocker fall. He looked around curiously, stroking his stringy beard with one hand and holding onto his cane with the other hand. No one answered. He dropped the knocker again. Still, no one answered. He tried the door, but it had been latched from the inside. "Hm!" he wondered. "That's strange!"

He walked around to the garden, where he saw Pavel playing in the dirt. He delivered a malicious smile, scaring the boy. He proceeded to enter the house from the rear door, mumbling to himself as he stepped over the threshold. Once he was inside with the door closed, he looked around. First, he entered Madeleine's room. "Hm. She has a vanity. A brush!" He proceeded to the opposite side, to Iakov's room, where he peeked inside and said to himself, "The old man's always sleeping. He'll never know I was here." He returned to the kitchen and walked to the mantel, where he noticed all the ornaments the Knesnoviches had collected over the years.

"Of course I have a right to enter this dwelling," he said to himself, examining the mantel. "After all, it's mine, as is all the contents."

He saw the gold medal, picked it up out of its cradle and sighed, "Ah!" victoriously. He clutched it to his chest with his hands and said, "The medal is mine, at last!" He stroked the singular strands of his beard again, thinking, "She'll never be able to pay her debts. I cannot destroy the house or this treasure will go down with it. I can sell this to the goldsmith in Soliere over the mountain for a fortune." He grinned with a greedy expression, and slipped the medallion around his neck. He looked around as he backed away. "This is my chance."

He decided his work was done and he went out the back way so no one would suspect he did anything unethical in the Knesnovich house. As he walked through the garden, Pavel tried to say something to him, but before the boy could finish, the landlord retorted, "Go learn to speak, boy!" Pavel stared at Mr. Robertson and the medallion that now hung around his neck, and started to mumble with tears mixed in with his unintelligible speech. Again, the dogs barked, but they did not deter Mr. Robertson from the business he intended to carry out.

CHAPTER 22

After Gilbert had been working in the shop for an hour, Oleg entered. She looked around until she had made sure that Gilbert noticed her.

"Pavel's playing in Madeleine's garden," Gilbert said, peeking beneath a tray on his worktable, noticing her grungy clothes.

"I know," Oleg said, winking back at him as she wiped her hands on her dress. "I saw him there."

"He loves to hang around there."

"I know, I know."

Gilbert continued his work while Oleg stood near the table. Every time he hammered the gray metal, she blinked her eyes, but she moved closer to the worktable. Gilbert looked up to face her, realizing how unkempt she appeared. He pulled his shoulders back when she spoke.

"What are you doing?" she asked.

"I am working on the riddle of the blight."

"You are wise," she said half smiling, pushing her dark hair back. "I know you can solve it."

"I'm going to try."

Gilbert continued to concentrate on his work while Oleg sat on a log to admire him. After a while, she strolled all around the work area, in restless motion, pushing wood fragments, making Gilbert uncomfortable.

"We are almost like husband and wife," she said coyly, intent on her mission. Only the horses occasionally distracted her.

Gilbert glanced at her over his shoulder and then at the room he had built, declining comment. He turned back to his bench work, picking up the metal for cursory examination. She tilted her head on another pass, failing to secure his full attention. He only gave a vague sense he was aware of her presence.

"We could be like that," Oleg suggested, twisting her lips with her finger. "There is a minister who could say the vows and write a document to make it legal."

"You don't understand my interest here," Gilbert said, caressing the metal piece.

"I think I do," Oleg said, smoothing her hands along her hips. "The boy needs a father." Gilbert looked around nervously as if seeking help. "I saw the way you looked at me."

"A man can never replace a boy's father."

"You are such a wise man, Gilbert. I am sure you can understand the wisdom in being a father to the boy."

"We are closer in age like brothers than father and son."

"You can teach him so much."

"That's all the more reason to have a brother image. He will look up to a brother better."

"Doesn't a man need a wife?" Gilbert stopped hammering. He regarded the log Pavel always sat on. He looked up at Madeleine's window, developing an adrenalin surge.

"He does," Gilbert said, as Oleg turned away with an angry expression, "but not this way." Her head snapped back to focus on his face.

"Aren't you a man?" she demanded.

"I am indeed," Gilbert confirmed. "That is all the more reason to be vigilant in uncertain situations."

"Of course, you must have discretion."

"It's not merely discretion. I have an obligation to myself."

"You keep to yourself because you are selfish."

"If I seem selfish, it is only to protect the creed the boy adheres to."

"Why is it you find a way to thwart every amorous gift I send to you?" Oleg cried. "You find ways to let me down." She dropped her head and sat again upon the log.

"It is not a put-down," Gilbert said. "I honor your womanhood by not taking advantage of your vulnerability." Oleg looked up at him with a glimmer of hope for her desires.

"I guess that is one reason I admire you so much. My husband was like that. A man of honor."

"He was?" Gilbert said, awkwardly.

"He was," Oleg admitted.

"It is getting dark," Gilbert said. "I will fetch the boy soon."

"Thank you."

"For what?"

"For honoring my boy."

Gilbert kept his smile all the time he prepared his bed in the wagon. As he crawled in, he saw she remained sitting outside the room on the log, looking out at the worktable.

Chapter 23

That night when Madeleine returned, the boy still played in the garden. He tried to explain what he saw, but his speech was so unintelligible Madeleine failed to understand him. When she entered her house, she saw Iakov was still sleeping. She began humming, recalling the happy tunes she sang along the way. She made a little fire in the hearth and put a kettle on her grate. As the water heated, she left the room, wandering back and forth from her room to the mantel. She started to imagine, *I shall have money to buy things. I need clothes.* She imagined Gilbert. She stepped to the mirror and pictured Gilbert at her side. "I will have the tailor make you a suit. You will have a top hat. Oh, you want a clean cotton shirt?" She bowed as though he were present. "Of course, my darling. I shall buy one for you. Anything you want, I can give you." She clutched her arms around her chest and closed her eyes and whispered with her lips pursed, "Only for you . . ."

Suddenly, the doorframe rattled and she heard the kettle whistling. The noise snapped her out of her reverie.

"What in the world are you doing, Madeleine?" Iakov said, observing her strange demeanor. "Are you trying to burn the house down?"

Madeleine immediately returned to reality, scampering back into the kitchen to prepare the tea. Her father rolled his chair to the kitchen table. Madeleine turned toward him, then glanced over at the mantel as though she were looking for something.

"Where did you go?"

"Father," she said, pulling her lips in. "I took your advice and visited Penelope and Marjorie." Iakov smiled as though he understood what transpired there. "They talked to me about the olden days."

"I suspected they would do that."

"They talked about Aunt Emma." Iakov smiled again, with an even wider grin. "You remember Aunt Emma, don't you, father?"

"I grew up with Emma."

"Then you know about her . . ."

"I know . . ."

"Well, they told me she's retired," Madeleine said, thoughtfully. "She could use help. Well, some help. I offered myself. You know what this means . . ."

"It means we can face Mr. Robertson." Iakov nodded as Madeleine moved away in thought, fidgeting with the teacups.

"Yes, it does."

Madeleine filled two cups with hot tea and joined her father. He reached over to her, placing his hand on top of hers, squeezing her fingers.

"Better days are coming," he assured. She regarded him with a gentle gesture, but somehow felt uncomfortable about the manner in which he expressed his words. Madeleine could tell he was concealing something. She glanced at the mantel again.

"Father," she said, reflecting on her first thoughts when she had returned home. "Did I leave something in your room?"

Iakov brought his hand slowly to his beard, turning his head slightly, gesturing with his eyebrows his lack of knowledge.

"I was asleep," he said. "I only heard the kettle's whistle."

"I was looking for something," Madeleine said in a dreamy state of mind. "I forgot what it was."

"Was it in the kitchen?"

"No," she said. "I thought I brought it in my room. There's nothing there."

"Maybe it is by the mantel, you're always putting things there."

"No, father. It wasn't something I put there. Something seems to be missing. I cannot tell what it is."

"Well, you'll find it when you remember what you took from there."

"That's just it, father. I didn't take anything from there." She shrugged her shoulders and stepped back toward the table, nearer to him.

"Well, look around, child."

Madeleine walked up to the mantel and gazed along the shelf, and experienced emptiness. "There's something missing, father," she realized, thinking about it for a long moment. She turned back to her room; she regarded the table. When she turned back to the mantel, she saw something different there making her approach it. She stared at it. She stepped up to it, squinting to see it.

"Father," Madeleine said, curiously. "There is a piece of parchment here. Strange I never noticed it before." She reached for it.

"See what it is, child."

"It has writing on it." She picked it up slowly.

"What does it say?"

"It says: 'Dear Madeleine, please forgive me for taking the metal, but it is an important part of the smelting work I will be doing. Believe me, it will fetch us a handsome sum. Always at your service, Gilbert.'" Madeleine turned to her father, who sat stiffly without speaking. She turned back to the mantel, looked it over, twitching her eyebrows in desperation. Her face broke into tears. She came to a realization, and screamed, "It's gone!"

"What's gone?" her father said.

"The medallion, father," she said, allowing her anxiety to show. She stared at the empty cradle that once held her father's precious trophy. She shivered, feeling abandoned and violated.

"What are you going to do, child?"

"I must face him, father."

She ran out of her house angrily, with her father calling after her. She scanned the yard until she found Pavel. She came over to him. "Where is Gilbert?" she demanded.

"Gil, Gil," Pavel tried to say, gesturing around his neck, "Lan, lan!"

"I have no time for this," Madeleine said, "Go home to your mother where you belong." The boy started to cry. He stood up and ran to Gilbert's shop. Madeleine followed. She found the shop door open. Gilbert had been experimenting with the nematodes when Madeleine made her presence known. She drew herself up, a fire blazing in her eyes.

"How could you?" she ranted, with tears streaming down both cheeks. "'At your service?'"

"You got my note . . ."

"Your note?" Madeleine said in a fiery tone. "What did you think you were doing?"

"I . . . I didn't think you'd mind," Gilbert said, hesitating. Her state of mind overwhelmed him. "I was just trying to help."

"Help?" Madeleine said. "By taking the medal that honors my family?"

"I didn't know it meant anything to you."

"That's what you think of my family's history and my father?"

"I thought it was just junk."

"You think my treasures are junk?" Madeleine released her emotions in a display of crying, with anger entwined with her tears.

"Come on, Madeleine. It's worthless!"

"Worthless?" she fired, regarding the floor while she contemplated. "I see your true nature now."

"Wait a minute," Gilbert said. "It's not like that."

"Oh?" Madeleine said. "What is it like?" Determination ruled her voice, giving her anger momentum.

"Madeleine!" Gilbert pleaded.

"Don't Madeleine me!" she shouted, her eyes glistening, swollen and wet. "Please don't come to our shanty again." Gilbert stared at her with an expression that showed a lack of understanding. "You are no longer welcome." She pulled away from him, putting her hands up protectively. The more he tried to advance, the more she backed away.

"But Madeleine . . ." She waved her hands above her head, indicating the end of their discussion. Her behavior left him with a helpless expression on his face. She exited and slammed the door behind her, making bird droppings fall from the crack in the roof.

Oleg opened her door after the crashing thrust of the big door's closing latch. She sat on a stool with her skirt pulled back to her calves. Her eyes were half-closed. She bore the expression of a woman who had been up dancing all night long.

"Now what was that all about?" Oleg demanded, in her groggy state. Gilbert remained defensively silent. He couldn't face her. Oleg tried again to get his attention. Gilbert displayed frustration and needed to explain his feelings, but not to Oleg.

"You look like you could use a friend," she said. Gilbert turned away, afraid to confront her. Pavel came out of the room, hanging around his mother. She turned to him.

"Why don't you go outside to play, Pavel." Pavel lunged at her with a grin.

"I play." He ran to where the horses were.

"You really look like you could use a friend!" she said again. She took out a little concertina and began to play it. Gilbert climbed back up on the wagon, acknowledging her with a simple look. He sat on the seat with his head in his hands and his elbows on his knees. The music was sweet and stimulating, making Gilbert tap his foot to the rhythm.

"I shouldn't be doing this," he said, climbing down from the rig, restlessly.

"Oh, c'mon," she said, and yanked him by the arm, making him fall onto her lap. Gilbert pulled himself up.

"Oleg, this is not right."

"I never saw a man decline the favors of a receptive woman."

"You are not a receptive woman. You are a woman alone."

"Are you telling me I'm desperate?" She began to play again.

When Madeleine came home, her father was already asleep. She was tired. She lay on her bed wondering what she had done to feel so dejected. "Why am I torturing myself?" she thought. "If he took it, there must be a reason. Would he just take it? Or is he trying to tell me something? Why must I be tortured about it?" She heard the music. "What is that?" she thought, and listened again. She firmed her expression and decided, looking up at the crack in the ceiling, "I must stop thinking about him. I would never let him ever have my heart! He can be plagued like everybody else in this hated place." She pulled up the covers and cried herself to sleep in the stillness of the overcast night.

During the night, it rained a little. Drops accumulated on her bed. When she rolled over, her leg found the wet spot. She awoke briefly, looked up to see the three-quarter moon shining down as the sky had cleared, and thought once again of the carpenter. She walked to the window in the kitchen, longing for just a glimpse of him, hoping to fill the void in her thoughts.

As she approached the window, she saw his lamp still on. When she saw him, she wondered if her eyes had deceived her. Gilbert passed by quite awake, as though he were dancing. She rubbed her eyes, making them burn as she struggled to see him, waiting, hoping he would pass by again. She saw Oleg. For a moment she felt anger, until she saw her pull him to her. Her anger transformed into rage. The pain she felt deep in her chest made her also feel sick. She felt as though someone had plunged a knife right through her heart. In an instant, her longing feelings had turned to hate. She knew she would never be able to relax this night. What she observed through her window robbed her of any joy she knew from earlier in the day. She returned to her room, lay in her bed, and shouted in the utmost despair, "I want to die!"

Chapter 24

Pavel woke up before the rooster's crow. When Gilbert climbed out of the canopy, he saw the boy squatting in front of his mother's door in an excited state. In moments, Oleg opened her door, surprising Pavel. She scratched her hair and then her legs. She looked up at the carpenter yawning and stretching.

"Doesn't look like Maddy's coming," she said in a sleepy voice, as Gilbert looked down at her.

"The way Madeleine reacted to me last night," Gilbert said. "I don't think she will bring us a food basket."

"Food basket," Pavel said with a smile, shaking his head. "Ya, ya, food. I hungry."

"The boy is hungry," Gilbert said.

Pavel pretended the stick with which he played was a wagon bouncing along the carriage road on the side of the mountain. He motioned with his hands how the doves and eagles flew over the wagon, making the sounds of the horses flapping their lips and neighing in defiance.

"Why don't I prepare a basket?" Oleg suggested. At first, Gilbert hesitated. He looked at Pavel. The boy's hunger was obvious to Gilbert and it bothered him even though the boy seemed to be quite occupied.

"That would be nice," he finally agreed.

Gilbert gave her some rubles to shop for bread, butter, milk and meal. In another hour, the two boys were outside, getting the wagon ready. Oleg called them back in to feed them. The three of them sat at Gilbert's worktable. Oleg watched over them as they consumed their breakfast. The horses waited outside the stable, hitched to the wagon, thrashing their manes, and stomping their restless feet. When they finished breakfast, Gilbert rested the implements against the outside wall in the bright sun.

"Gil, Gil," Pavel cried, looking up at the mountain. "I see metal."

"Yeah," Gilbert promised, as he also looked up the slope. "We're going up the mountain with the wagon to get the metal."

"No, Gil," Pavel said. "Lan, lan."

"It's a big land. We'll take the horses."

"No, lan," he tried to say with a tiring expression.

"Yes, lan," Gilbert said, ignoring the significance of Pavel's broken speech. "Let's get the reins."

"Horse!" Pavel said, pointing to the big animal. Pavel's excitement about the journey showed in his behavior. Gilbert perceived a boy excited about an adventure, even though he mentioned the landlord often.

"If we can bring back enough ore," Gilbert promised, "we will start smelting tomorrow. By then we'll have a fine culture to rid Auguliere of these horrendous insects." Pavel smiled.

Pavel helped Gilbert load pickaxes, shovels and Johnson bars. The grubs did not damage hardwood tools. He kept the tools in a bed of pine resin to protect them. Pavel brought the bridles to Gilbert to finish hitching up the horses. In another few minutes, the boy climbed up on the buckboard seat, next to Gilbert. Gilbert hugged him protectively. The boy became silent in the warmth of Gilbert's arms. Gilbert saw the boy's happiness in his presence. Madeleine watched them from her window.

They drove away from the stable, along the main cobblestone street to the market square and up the dirt road out to the North Slope, leaving a trail of dust. The wagon bounced along the deep gullies, making the tools rattle. They climbed the mountain until the village became a distant group of dwellings. The dwellings drew a more compact form as they progressed, until they appeared as a clump in the huge expanse of the valley. They stopped the wagon in the wonderful high country breeze to admire the view. Gilbert saw the switchbacks of the carriage road. The road had grown seedy and was covered in places with tall grass. The high carriage wheels enabled the horses to pull the carriage on the road. The animals stepped in the bare spots in the ruts along the way. The cliff was easy to climb, taking them up onto the scree slope. This area was strewn with small rocks and occasionally a bolder. Another hundred yards led them to hoof marks from his previous ride. Gilbert parked the wagon there. They continued up the scree slope on foot. They followed the hoof marks to the gray area. Once there, they looked down at the carriage road, but the horses and wagon were hidden from view.

Gilbert saw how excited Pavel was to accompany him on this journey. Gilbert thought about this. He felt sorry for Pavel who had no brother to show him the meaning of being a boy. Neither did he have a father to guide him.

After two hours, the trail made switchback turns climbing the scree slope. They passed a grove of pines. The trail ended at the foot of a cliff. Gilbert had tied a rope around Pavel to protect him while he climbed up the cliff. Once on top, he fixed the rope so it would serve as a pulley to lower bags of the metal down to the base of the cliff.

"It sure is funny that people have to fight for nothing," Gilbert thought aloud. Pavel clutched Gilbert's hand and looked up at him as he would a big, protective brother. His smile gave Gilbert a good feeling. Pavel was still excited. All this was new to him. Gilbert loved to watch Pavel as he discovered the new world which surrounded him. Even for Gilbert, it was a rediscovery. He had forgotten just how majestic it was. The last time he had come up here, Madeleine distracted him. Now he thought of her differently. He struggled with her rejection. Pavel was one of the few excuses he had to rationalize his indifference. However, he needed his work to take his mind completely off the fruitless pursuit.

The memories were still fresh in his mind. Each time he stepped on the ground in the gray area, he was reminded of possibilities. When he found pieces of the gray metal and compared them to the ingot he carried, he couldn't help think there were other forces at work. Maybe he needed to find out. Maybe he didn't know where to start. Maybe he should talk to Vladimir. He knew everything. Maybe he knew a secret.

Both Gilbert and Pavel worked to remove as much ore as possible. Gilbert swung the pick into the rock, shattering large fragments of stone. When he moved on to a new area, Pavel shoveled the gray rock pieces into piles. Later both examined the contents of each pile, only throwing the richest ore into the sacks. It was a long haul to the wagon. They made numerous trips to the wagon, dumping the rich ore. When they loaded a half a ton, Gilbert called to the boy, "We have a full load, Pavel. Let's take her down." The boy squinted in the bright sunlight, smiling. His exuberant pride billowed from his face. He climbed onto the wagon as though he were the wagon-master.

"Who is 'her?'" Pavel asked. "Is it Madeleine?"

"No, Pavel," Gilbert said, stepping up, nearer to the boy. "The wagon is called 'her.'"

"I know why," Pavel insisted, sliding down the slope on his feet. "Cause you love her . . ." Then, Pavel giggled when he stopped just short of Gilbert.

They ate lunch that Oleg had packed for them, sitting amongst the pieces of ore in the high country, feeling the fresh mountain breezes. It was quiet, except for a solitary eagle carried aloft on warm rising currents high on the pitch. Pavel watched the creature soar, wondering how it flew. He imitated the flight motions with his hands, pretending he was an eagle, and giggled as he portrayed it. Gilbert was honored to participate in his discoveries. Yet, he was reminded of Madeleine with everything he did.

Late in the afternoon, when the two horses pulled the heavy load down the mountain, the two zinc miners arrived at Gilbert's shop with their load of ore. Oleg came out of the stable when she heard the wagon pull up to the door. She let the big door swing open. Gilbert grabbed Larson by his bushy mane and whispered, “C’mon, boy. Bring ’er in.” Oleg stood in a lazy stance, leaning against the door to hold it open as the animals dragged the ore load safely inside. Before she closed the big door, Gilbert caught a glimpse of Madeleine’s cart and pony as she brought it through the alleyway to her garden. Madeleine kept an unemotional expression on her face the whole time, and made Gilbert feel disconnected from her. It was the first time the carpenter felt utterly helpless in her presence, and it made him want to change her perception of him. How?

Chapter 25

Ever since Gilbert went out into the meadows for nematodes, and up on the hillside for ore, his evenings were filled with shop work. Madeleine knew this because she saw his lamp's illumination through her window. She remembered looking for her father through the window in the later hours when he was productive.

"The question is," Iakov said, wheeling himself into the kitchen after Madeleine had returned from work one evening, "was it worth it?" Madeleine felt the shadow of ambivalence once again invading her peace. She turned to confront her father, knowing the spirit of his mood.

"I know that look," Madeleine said.

"You know nothing."

"Then why do I feel like I'm at the table with you and mother?"

"Mother left her mark, she did."

"Oh, and what did she always tell the children?"

"I think she always said you have to trust your heart," Iakov said. Madeleine frowned and nodded in agreement. Iakov lowered his head in an effort to look under her frown. "So what does your heart tell you now?" Madeleine leaned over and held her father's hand, lifting her head so he saw her sullen expression.

"It tells me I'm confused," Madeleine said. She brought his work-worn hands up to her face, to caress her cheek with the sprigs of stiff hair standing on the back of his hand.

"Maybe he had a good reason. Is he really an evil man?" She bit her lower lip, allowing one tear to form.

"No, father," she clarified, wiping her eye with the free hand. "He's not an evil man." She held back some sniffles. "Is that why I feel so guilty?" Her voice quavered.

"No, child. You feel guilty because you have a tender heart, just like your mother."

"Then what does it show? What must I do now?"

"It shows you have feelings."

"I thought I did the right thing, father." She felt betrayed by her decision.

"Yes, child. You had to do what your heart told you at that moment."

"By now I have made him feel less of a man."

"You do not have to justify your deeds."

"Yet, he is strong. He can overcome this. Therefore, he doesn't need me." Iakov took his hand back, pulled out his cotton handkerchief and offered it to Madeleine. She took the soft cloth and cried profusely into it. "No," she said, still sobbing. "He surely doesn't need me. Aunt Emma only needs me to do her bidding. I have no purpose."

"I need you, Madeleine."

"You need me to take care of you, father."

"No," Iakov insisted. "You may never fully understand just how much I need you. Until my job is done, I need you." She scratched her head in bewilderment.

"Oh, father!" she cried, "I am sorry to speak to you in such a harsh way. What shall I do?"

"You must listen to your heart and reconcile your indecisions."

"You are so wise, father. I am so stupid."

"You are not stupid, child." He came close, lifted his frail hand and picked up her chin gently.

"You are beautiful with a bosom full of love. You have the sane knowledge to know what to do. I have raised you well."

"Yes, father. You have. I shall yet make you proud of me."

"That you will, my child."

Madeleine retreated to her room, tired from working all day and crying most of the evening. She knew what Gilbert was doing with Pavel but her embarrassment prevented her from speaking to him. She waited, however, to see his light in the night so she felt safe in her heart.

Chapter 26

By the time Pavel returned to the stable, night had fallen. The lamp burned in the grungy corner, barely illuminating the work area. The shop lay still. Only on occasion, a mouse scampered along the floor against the wall until it found a hole into which to run. Even the horses were quiet. Gilbert worked on the cultures. The shelves on the wall adjacent to the hearth were stacked with racks of cultured nematodes. Pavel tugged Gilbert's pants as he looked up at the dozen trays, saying, "Todes, todes." Gilbert knew Pavel experienced a certain joy in working on these things. They were boy activities. He never had the chance to have these experiences with his mother. After his father was killed in an accident, his mother found herself overprotective. This disenchanted the boy. Gilbert rejuvenated these feelings in the boy's heart.

In the morning, Gilbert sat Pavel down on the log to show him the plan. Oleg watched, sipping her morning tea.

"We are going to inoculate the infested wood with nematodes."

" 'Noculate," Pavel said.

"Inoculate," Gilbert clarified.

He helped Gilbert load the trays into the wagon and covered them with his wool blanket. Pavel patted the top of the blanket, the way a father tucks in his son.

"Todes warm," he said, expressing his joyful satisfaction through his wonderful smile. Gilbert nodded with the same joy on his face.

He climbed up, then Pavel climbed up after him, sitting beside him. Gilbert grabbed the reins.

"Yaw!" Gilbert screamed.

Pavel laughed as the wagon jounced along. Gilbert drove the wagon slowly on the cobblestones and even slower on the dirt roads lined with deep gullies. They headed westward to the chicken farms down in the valley, where the mountain stream flowed, and the high grassland and tea plantations greeted them.

In the distance, they heard the relentless cackling of chickens and occasionally a rooster's crow rattled them. Gilbert knew they neared Mr. Winthrop's farm when they smelled the smoke of a wood-burning fire.

A wind came down the slope from the icy mountaintop, mixing with the moist warm air in the valley, making fog clouds billow up from the flowing water. From far down the valley, the fog appeared like a white veil over the low-lying land.

The farmer charged out of his house and recognized Gilbert's wagon right away. His face grew raw with anger and he walked toward the wagon with clenched fists.

"What you doin' out here, mister?" the farmer said.

"Please let me help," Gilbert said. "I hold a cure for the infestation."

The farmer approached the wagon with a skeptical face, examined Gilbert's load and glanced at the boy.

"Ain't that Oleg Chernyshev's boy?"

"He's helping me with the nematodes."

"Todes!" Pavel yelled with glee.

"What in the world is that?"

"That is the cure," Gilbert said. "They are tiny creatures that eat the beetle grub."

"How can they do that?" the farmer said. "Lemme see 'em."

"You can't see them," Gilbert said.

"What kind of joke do you play with me, stranger?" the farmer said, raising his hands in the air.

"Need glass," Pavel said.

"What's the child talkin' 'bout?"

"The boy's right," Gilbert said. "You do need a glass to see them. They are what we call microscopic."

"Don't go pullin' them big words on me, mister. You think you are the landlord?"

"No," Gilbert said. "I am not. I want to help. The landlord was the one who infected the village."

"How you know that?"

"I cannot explain how he did it, but I know he managed to spread these beetles in all the new wood. They eat some of the old wood, too."

"How do you use those 'todes' of yours?"

"Nematodes," Gilbert said. "We put some on the larvae and in a couple of days you will see them die."

"That so?" said the farmer. "What happens to them after the grubs are gone?"

"The nematodes move on to find other grubs and do the same."

"You have a convincing argument," the farmer said, "but how can I trust you?"

"Trust does have to be earned," Gilbert said, "but you have to give me the chance to earn it. Why would I want to lie about this?"

"That is true," the farmer said. "You seem to have the wisdom of an elder, although you are young."

"I have traveled far with my father."

"I see you are not from here," the farmer said. "Your face is clean and your hair is light, like hay."

"No, I am not."

"You did honest work on the coops. Maybe you tell some truth."

"What have you got to lose?" Gilbert pleaded.

"When you put it that way, I am concerned. I do indeed need help."

"I love Auguliere. I would never harm this place. I have found treasures here that cannot be found anywhere on earth."

"A man that sounds sincere must be sincere. That's what my pappie always said."

"Your father is wise."

"My father passed his life."

"I am sorry for that," Gilbert said.

"No need." The farmer shook his head and spat. "He's there because he failed to heed his own advice."

"Many of us do that."

"You may use your nematodes," the farmer said. "How do we start?"

Gilbert lifted out a tray and placed it on the edge of the wagon. He lifted the cover. The farmer gaped at the tray's contents.

"All I see is dirt," the farmer said. Gilbert dug into the dirt with his hands."

"Ich! Grub," Pavel yelled, making a face. He placed the grub on the wagon's wood.

"It's just a grub, Pavel."

"It's kinda' run down, ain't it?" the farmer said.

"That's because it is infected with nematodes," Gilbert said. The farmer scratched his head studying the situation.

"We'll put some of this dirt on your wood and you'll see results in a few days. We'll put some in the barn where I replaced sides with the aspen boards."

The two men and the boy worked to spread the nematode-laden dirt among infested areas.

"Now go down to old man Abram's. His shanty is about to fall down."

Mr. Abrams was just as resistant at first. Gilbert managed to convince him it was best. He tried to inoculate the entire valley with the nematodes. A few of the farmers declined treatment of their wood. Enough of them, however, were treated so the nematodes would circulate all over Auguliere.

In addition, Gilbert inoculated his shop and the park, where the trees grew.

A few days later, farmers came to Gilbert's shop to thank him. Several days after that, the plague of the beetles started to lift and once again residents greeted the handsome, young carpenter with the respect he once enjoyed.

In the time that followed, Gilbert rebuilt the shanties whose wood the beetles weakened. He had forged big bolts out of the zinc. He had also made wing nuts, which twisted at the end of the bolt, holding it in place in the wood. The soft zinc allowed the sharp edges of the nuts to cut the metal to form threads, locking it in place. He used his brace to bore holes in the wood. He slipped the bolts through the holes and locked the pieces together. Gilbert continued to work every day and gradually, Auguliere returned to the way it was before the blight.

All the while Madeleine watched him forging the metal, and the relationship he developed with Pavel. Madeleine started to cry as she watched him. She knew something was missing, but she lacked the fortitude to confront Gilbert again. She only sat by the window and watched the handsome man accomplish his daily work with the boy. She never saw the medallion, and she wondered what had become of it.

Iakov had wheeled himself into the kitchen one evening when Madeleine returned from Emma's. He looked up at her as she watched, forlorn.

"Try to think of the good in his heart," Iakov said

"You startled me, father."

"Sometimes we need a jolt to make us realize our surroundings."

"I am getting bored of my surroundings."

"I know, child."

"Are you trying to have me open my heart again?"

"Your heart is yours to decide what to do with."

"You would say that, father."

"You will know when it is time to give it."

"So that I can allow him to break it?"

"Oh, child," Iakov said. "You are my most precious treasure. Far more precious than any medal can be."

"Father," Madeleine finally said. "What are you telling me to do?"

"I cannot tell you any more, Madeleine. You are as much a woman as your mother was. Only you can decide what to do."

She reflected on those warm days with her mother. She saw in visions how her mother prepared the table, how she took great pride to make sure the house was adequately prepared for the family. The thought also made her feel inadequate, trying to compare herself with her mother. Once again, Madeleine retreated to the silence of her room to cry.

CHAPTER 27

The landlord stood next to his buckboard on the street regarding Mrs. Teivel's shop with awe, as he poised himself to enter. "My first deed must be to ferret out the strength of that carpenter. I beseech you, assist me, advisor." He opened the flimsy door, and stepped up to the front of the big counter. She stood once more to face Mr. Robertson. He did not have to speak. She knew what was on his mind.

"Beetles did the job just right, now his metal's milling . . . He finds a way to deal with blight, an amalgam controls his building."

Mr. Robertson regarded her with the curiosity of a child, attempting to see what she was up to. She turned away, keeping her secrets to herself by fidgeting with jars, containers, and other items on her shelves. Finally, she pulled out a strange vial of silver liquid. The way she handled it, the liquid sloshed around in an alien way. She came to the counter with it, and poured some into a smaller vial.

"What is this?"

"It is a medium to alter the state of the carpenter's gray metal." She looked at the landlord, squinting with her good eye. "When he tries to screw each bolt, It pours like tea from a kettle. It will undermine his work, and melt his precious metal."

She stared at him with a stolid expression as though her face were made of metal, gleaming and hard. When he continued to gawk at her, confused, she hammered her fists on the counter.

"To make it work without a quirk, I need five hundred rubles, sir."

"Five hundred rubles?" the landlord bellowed. "I don't carry that kind of money around."

Her eye was glazed with an ascetic cloak. She bent over the counter to be directly in front of him, challenging him with her pose. She coughed several times, barely catching her breath, but remained steadfast.

"You pay me or perish!" For the first time, he feared her. She held up the vial for him to touch.

"What is this?" the landlord asked. "What kind of potion gleams so well?"

"We call it liquid silver," she said.

"Liquid silver!" the landlord said. "I will have to return to my house to obtain that sum."

"Hurry!" she said, withdrawing behind the counter. "Time is running out!"

Mr. Robertson departed the store, climbed onto his wagon and rode back to the West Slope. When he arrived at the house, he left the buckboard where it stopped. He entered. The cat greeted him. He pushed her aside, walked directly to his cache and retrieved enough currency to satisfy Mrs. Teivel's hunger. As he opened the door to his bedroom, the hinges fell off, and the heavy oak structure almost collapsed on top of him. When he opened the drawer, he saw those same black beetles and dozens of eggs. "How did these things get here?" he said to himself. He looked around in the empty house as if to summon help, but he was alone except for the cat.

"What in high hill's name is this?" he mumbled, letting his fingers wrestle with the strands of his beard. "How did these creatures find their way into my abode?" He walked out of the house and said to himself, "I must get back to Mrs. Teivel's." He glanced up at the clouds as they began to darken, high up in the valley. He climbed up on the old rig and settled himself in the seat. He whipped the reins and the team started to pull the load down the trail.

When he returned to Mrs. Teivel's shop, he found she was not there. Someone had left the door open. "Where could she be now? Come to think of it, I have never known her not to be there. This is strange indeed," he said out loud to himself. "I shall have to return later. I wonder where she is?"

He stepped into the alley beside the store and marched to its end. He turned into the courtyard where he found the outhouse. "I wonder if she's in here." At first, he hesitated, not wanting to disturb her there. His impatience prevailed and he pulled open the heavy oak door. When he surveyed the space, a puzzled expression crossed his face.

"Hm!" he said, scratching his scrawny beard as he gazed at the empty seat. "Now where could this woman be?"

He felt the shadow of someone standing behind him as he gazed into the vacated backhouse. He hesitated to turn even though he knew he had to face his pursuer before he could escape from the alley. The possibility of having to confront Mrs. Teivel horrified him, as he stepped back just far enough to close the door. In an awkward attempt to turn, he caught a glimpse of the stalker. He sighed with relief when he realized that the old woman would not have the chance to scorn him here.

"What on earth are you doing snooping around the latrine?" the woman demanded.

She stood gazing at him, adjusting her feathered hat and moving in her fitted dress. Mr. Robertson gulped and hesitated again in reaction to the familiar face. He moved further away, glancing at the closed door several more times before he could face her again.

"I was just checking to see where that cat went that I chased into the alleyway," he assured.

"Cat?" she posed. "Since when are you tracking the stray cats of Auguliere?"

"My concern for cats is no secret?"

"Only when you are behind Mrs. Teivel's shop."

The adrenalin that surged in his stomach put a sickly feeling in his mind. He needed to fire back comments to her, but somehow he lost the fortitude to spar with her. When he swung himself around to walk past her, he realized the nature of the confrontation and that she was not readily letting him pass.

"I have business to attend to, Raisa," he admitted.

She appeared to let him pass, making it clear to him that he would have to brush by her. He inched along, purposely trying to avoid physical contact, but it was inevitable. She took the opportunity to stare him in the eye as they passed, face to face. She smiled with her lips together and remained as dignified as before. She only continued to focus on him as he backed out of the narrow way until he could see her no more.

Feeling frustrated, he returned to the front door of the shop, where he saw no evidence that Mrs. Teivel had returned. He waited until Raisa stepped back out onto the street before he entered the shop again. He hammered his fists on the counter, but heard no response. He decided to take a bold step behind the counter, locate the liquid silver on the rack and help himself to it. Sweat formed on his brow as he considered the theft. He held up the vial and thought, "Now I can finally put an end to this carpenter's deeds." His thoughts provided comfort in that at last he thought he had the ability to stunt the carpenter's work, even though he was not sure just how.

He climbed back on the buckboard, shook the reins and the team pulled the big wagon along. The people that he saw in the streets reminded him that he maintain a certain amount of vigilance to spare him of the embarrassment he might have if Mrs. Teivel spotted him now.

Chapter 28

The landlord returned to his house, where he planned how he would carry out his deed. The cat jumped up on his lap as he sat at his table with his tea.

"So, I shall go into the night and place a new plague on the carpenter's metal. I shall do it on the night of the full moon instead of collecting taxes. That way, no one will suspect anything." He held the cat with one hand, clutching the liquid silver with the other as he contemplated his mission. "How do I make this potion work? How do I make this material complete its task?" He wondered and debated, and considered revisiting Mrs. Teivel's shop. It occurred to him that she could have expired. "Maybe she met her own end in some horrible way that I would care not to witness? Or, perhaps I will never know her secret?"

Some people observed his odd activity near buildings the carpenter had repaired, but they chose not to ask him what he intended. Fear always prevented people from confrontations with the landlord and consequently drove them away. His deeds did create gossip. He continued to snoop around, causing suspicion among the townspeople, well into the night. He poked at the metal the carpenter smelted from the ore right in his own shop. Finally, he dumped the entire contents of the liquid silver in the container. When he finished, he scampered away like a thief in the night, but not without certain people observing his buckboard heading up the trail to his house.

The next day, he never came back to town. Vladimir came to Madeleine looking for the landlord. Madeleine didn't understand why Vladimir wanted to know, but her father knew. When he learned the night of the full moon loomed, and the landlord was missing, he folded his arms over his chest as a sign.

Madeleine opened her eyes from her nap as the heavy knocker sounded. When she realized it was her door and not a dream, she dragged herself from her room and opened the big door. Vladimir stood at the threshold with a concerned look.

"Come in, Vladimir. I will make some tea." Vladimir didn't answer. Madeleine put the kettle on the hearth and stoked the smoldering embers, adding some kindling. "You look like you have the weight of the world on your shoulders," she called over her shoulder.

"I have the weight of the town." The kindling magically burst into flame, drawing Vladimir's attention.

"Pull up a chair," Madeleine said. Vladimir sat next to Madeleine at her table.

"Hm!" her father vocalized from his room. Madeleine peeked in to see her father, half awake with his arms by his side.

"I don't know if Mr. Robertson ever returned home last night," Vladimir said.

"Why do you say that?"

"Because I didn't see him at the town hall today."

"Neither did I," Madeleine said. "I pass by the market every morning."

"He should have come by the clerk's office the day after tax collection."

"Why are you so concerned?"

"Last night was the night of the full moon. You know what that means."

"So, doesn't he use the buckboard?"

"Not last night," Vladimir said, standing and admiring her mantel.

"I don't wish bad things on people."

"He can be foolish. He is often blinded by his own greed."

"Uh!" Iakov sighed.

"Father?" Madeleine called. Vladimir removed his hat and adjusted himself in his chair at the table. Iakov did not answer Madeleine's call. "Father?" she called again, looking over her shoulder, with a greater urgency in her voice. "Let me see if father fell asleep again." She stood, brushing crumbs from her dress, and walked to his bed. Vladimir struggled to see. She noticed his arms crossed over his chest. For a moment, she thought *his arms were straight before*. She pinched her lips together in discomfort. Vladimir stood up in a nervous pose.

"Is anything wrong?" Madeleine remained preoccupied. Vladimir tried to look on.

"Father," she called softly, staring at his blank face. She gently shook him, leaning over him. "Father?" she called again. He remained quiet. Vladimir still looked on, stepping closer, realizing that something was indeed wrong.

Madeleine looked back at Vladimir with a worried, contorted face. She looked again at Iakov's placid face and motionless body. "Father!" she cried again, clutching one of his hands. She stepped back and fell to her knees. The man never moved, but his eyelids were partly opened in an uncharacteristic way. This frightened her. She realized that he had expired.

"Father!" she screamed. Once again, "Father!" she cried, sobbing between bouts of crying. Iakov never answered.

Torrents of fresh tears swept over her face, dripping down her cheeks until they joined the corners of her mouth. Her tongue sampled their salty taste. "Oh, father," Madeleine cried, "You can't leave me now." She put her hand to her mouth. She surmised what her father had meant, "*This means your job is done . . .*" She pushed her hands into his chest, letting her brown hair flow all over his gray beard and breathless mouth, "No, no! Your job is not done," she pleaded with him. "No, father, no! You can't leave me now. Not now!" Iakov's lifeless body refused to respond to her, and her worst fear came to life.

Vladimir reached over to close Iakov's eyes. Madeleine continued to cry uncontrollably. For the first time in all her twenty years, she realized she may no longer have him to talk to. She sat on the edge of the bed, wondering how life would be without him. She found Marjorie and Penelope in her mind, nagging her, making her revisit those awful days of subjugation and terror. They always had to tease her, always took away the little bits of mother's memory she had to hang onto. Now she stood bare, alone in the hostile world, afraid to put her next foot forward. She was at the end, with the loss of her salvation.

She wondered if her sisters were going to prevail, if they were going to insist she shoulder the expense of the funeral. She felt the threat of those sisters as if they were in the same room with her. *Why should we pay? He never visited us!*

"No!" Madeleine shouted as she stood, startling Vladimir.

"Madeleine," Vladimir said, snapping Madeleine back to reality. "You had better sit down. Do you want me to bring someone? Your friends, your sisters?"

"No!" Madeleine shouted again. "Not them. I don't want to see them."

"They may want to see their father."

"Then they can, but I don't have to embrace them, at least not with my heart."

"No, you don't have to see them."

"I don't know what I want . . ." She picked up her apron, but found no tears to wipe.

"Sh!" Vladimir hushed, taking her hand again.

"What am I going to do now? I'm going to be so lost without him."

"You will find a way. Iakov gave you a strong spirit."

"Then why do I feel so weak?" she said with renewing sobs.

"What about the carpenter?"

"Oh, how can I face him now? He's probably laughing at me. Should I make myself out to be a bigger fool?"

"You only feel weak now because you are vulnerable."

She knelt again, and looked deeply into Iakov's face, searching it for answers, saying, "Why?" Vladimir knew she saw a man at peace. He grabbed her shoulders and raised her slowly from her crouch. She burst into tears again as she let him absorb her with his arms. Vladimir took her head in his hands as though to shield her from death. Vladimir could not stop her from gazing at him. Her tears dripped down and merged with saliva dripping from her quavering lips. She stared at him, while Vladimir still held onto her.

"No . . . why must this happen now? Why?"

Vladimir brought her back to the table, and sat her down again. He explained to her he would help arrange the burial. Vladimir looked away from Madeleine for a moment, recalling his own problem.

Later in the day, Oleg came out of her door to find the carpenter and the boy completely absorbed in their own world. She walked around, sat on her log and still neither had noticed her. Even when she cleared her throat the metal clanking drowned out Oleg's communication attempts. She only took their attention when she swung Gilbert's huge ax into a chunk of wood. Gilbert dropped his tools, and ran to her.

"You have to be careful with that," he said. "I've seen people lose their fingers or even a hand." She looked up at him in a half smile, letting her eyes blink more often than normal. She still bore a sleepy expression as Gilbert stood over her. He took the ax from her hand and leaned it against the wall.

"Did you hear all the commotion next door? Sounds like they're having a party."

"I don't think so," Gilbert said. "Madeleine doesn't have parties."

"See for yourself. Have you ever seen four wagons hitched up in front of the Knesnovich residence?" Gilbert glanced through the window and saw well-dressed people inside. "Iakov Knesnovich is a very influential man. Maybe someone has come from afar to greet him and Maddy?"

"I don't know," Gilbert said.

"There's a lot of activity," Oleg said. "You've only known the girl for a few months. What do you really know about her? Besides, I saw Vladimir run in and out a few times."

"They're friends . . ."

"Sure they are . . ."

"Oh, there's nothing going on," Gilbert insisted. Oleg gave the carpenter a look that made him think again. "Is there?"

"Only one way to find out," Oleg assured.

"She told me to never again come to her house. I must honor her request."

Gilbert watched two men remove the heavy casket from the Knesnovich house. It did not occur to him that it carried Iakov Knesnovich. "Maybe they sold their house and had to move out." When he saw several women, he thought, "She's moving into her sisters'." Oleg shook her head and shrugged her shoulders.

"Maybe she lost her house to the landlord?" she suggested.

The mystery of the gathering bothered Gilbert. Oleg had never seen him so fidgety before. He remained in the shop, unable to ascertain the nature of the gathering.

In the meantime, Madeleine held onto Vladimir's hand on the right with Agafon clutching her arm on the left. As she walked out of the shanty and stepped into the waiting buggy, she stopped for a moment and glanced back affectionately at Gilbert's shop. She executed an abrupt turn, and climbed the rest of the way into the coach. Agafon climbed into the coach after her and sat beside her.

"Do you want me to advise him?" Agafon asked.

"No," Madeleine said. "He has enough of his own worries."

She heard the driver call to the mules, and felt the animals pull the carriage away from her house. It drove off to the east on the cobblestone road. Gilbert peeked out of the stable to see the carriage disappear over the hill.

CHAPTER 29

Days later, Gilbert started complaining about the zinc's quality. Pavel played with the zinc ingots in the basket, agitating Gilbert, making him react to the boy in a way he had not done before.

"What are you doing?" Gilbert snapped. "What did you do to this metal?" Pavel recoiled from Gilbert's acrid tone, displaying guilt on his face. Gilbert turned back to the worktable, picked up a piece of the gray metal and wondered. "That's strange," he said to Pavel, who had slipped closer to him, despite the carpenter's sharp remarks. "This metal was placed in this container two days ago when it was freshly smelted. It should be gray now. Why are some of the pieces shiny?" Pavel picked up the piece to look at it as if he really knew why it was shiny.

"It's shiny, Gil," he said, testing the surface of it with his fingers.

"Yes," Gilbert said, realizing Pavel was correct. "It is. I wonder why?"

The sun hid behind giant cumulus clouds in the crisp fall air, making the carpenter and the boy lazy. Gilbert welcomed this weather. It soothed him in the late hours of the day, when he stopped to take a break. He remembered the days when

Madeleine came by the shop with those tasty little treats. He glanced now and then at her window, bearing a forlorn expression. Others came to distract him from the laziness of the late afternoon. Although Vladimir had been a regular fixture, Agafon also came by the shop just to check on the carpenter's well-being, but Vladimir failed to appear the last three days. Instead, Gilbert saw him visit Madeleine often.

Agafon entered the shop quietly, gaping around to catch him off-guard, but Gilbert sensed his presence. It was hard to fool him. He seemed to know his surroundings at all times. Only the landlord truly caught him off-guard. He had an agenda for which Gilbert had not been prepared.

"We finally got some of our clouds back, my friend," Agafon yelled.

"Agafon," Gilbert yelled back from his bench. "Good to see you."

Agafon took his hat off and joined him in the shop, offering some bread his wife had baked. Gilbert took the succulent treat, acknowledging Agafon with gratitude.

"Cuttin' some wood as usual," Agafon said. "Maybe someday every board in Auguliere will bear your mark, much the way old Iakov Knesnovich had made his mark. You're younger and more full of spirit."

"If only that were true." Gilbert bolstered a laugh.

"It's true, my friend. You have the mark of an immortal." Agafon said. "How 'bout some tea?"

"Not a bad idea," Gilbert said. "Shall I put the kettle on the hearth?" Gilbert smiled quietly, going about his chores of picking up the kettle and stuffing a few small cut logs amongst the smoldering embers. Yet, in the deep reaches of his mind, he couldn't help imagine Madeleine's soft hand always near. He returned with his face aimed at the ground.

"I know that look. Something heavy must be on your mind," Agafon said.

"You can read it on my face?"

"Indeed, man!" Agafon said. "There are many things a man can hide, but not that feeling for a special woman."

"Then it really shows."

"What really shows is your willingness to accept things as they are."

"It's not as if I have a choice about it," Gilbert said. "She thinks I have done unspeakable things. You know how much she loves her father."

"Why not tell her?"

"I cannot even get close to the house. Besides, I haven't seen her in days."

"I know you've lived a good life and are a decent man."

"How can you know if a man lived a good life?"

"How does any man know a man lived a good life?"

"You must examine his whole life," Gilbert said. "You can only do that when his life is finished."

"It is too late for him."

"It is," Gilbert said, "for *him*."

"Ah, yes!"

"My father taught me to do good work and to hold your head up high and feel proud."

"So, what's wrong with that?" Agafon said.

"There are people in this world who are jealous of your accomplishments. They will look to break them down if they cannot compete."

"So?"

"So, it is far better to soothe your foe with humility rather than provoke him with your pride."

"Are you going to try to soothe him when he comes around to collect his rent?"

"I have to pay the rent."

"Are you prepared for it to be doubled?"

"I'll do what I have to."

"If the landlord thinks you are earning any money, he will triple it."

"When does he come?"

"The moon was full three days ago. He should have come on the buckboard."

"I thought he walked to the village?"

"Not on the full moon. That's when the wolves are out."

"Madeleine warned me about the wolves. The moon's not full now."

"It's only dangerous on the road. Once you're in the village it's safe."

The men sat, talking about the landlord and discussing the full moon for hours. Gilbert was showing off his accomplishment to Agafon when the broad door was suddenly flung open. Vladimir came running into the shop. His eyes were big and watery. He wore an unusually serious tone on his face. Gilbert pressed toward him as he entered the work area.

"Vladimir, what is the trouble?" Gilbert said. "You look like you're running from a ghost."

"I have two things to tell," he said.

"I've never seen you so upset, Vladimir," Agafon said. "What is bothering you?" Agafon regarded Vladimir with an inquisitive expression.

"First, I must sadly report Iakov Knesnovich is dead."

"No!" Gilbert said. Agafon sighed with relief. His secret was finally released.

"I never had a bad wish for Madeleine," Gilbert said.

"She must know that," Agafon said.

"You said you have two things to tell," Gilbert said.

"It's my father. I must find him."

"Your father?" Gilbert said. "You never even told me you have a father."

"Just come with me. I will explain on the way."

"Let me come also," Agafon said. They took Gilbert's wagon. On the way, Vladimir told his story.

"There was a wealthy family. Many years ago, before there was a village, there was a dream. My great-grandfather had a dream." Both Agafon and Gilbert listened intently as the wagon bounced along the dirt road. "There was everything to live for. The hills were filled with the infamous gray metal you see displayed on every door."

"How did that come about?" Gilbert wondered.

"There was a huge smelting operation with the help of nearby towns and the city of La Grange. Giant mills were built there. My grandfather had big plans." Vladimir wiped his face with his sleeve. "The family was plagued with disease."

"How terrible," Gilbert said.

"When the mines were closed and the mining operation halted, my father started the tea plantation." Gilbert fingered his chin.

"That explains why everyone in Auguliere . . ."

"My father was the only grandson. As a result, he inherited everything. My mother died at my birth, leaving me an orphan. There was no doctor in Auguliere and she hemorrhaged. So you see, my father is the landlord." Gilbert's face showed shock.

"What do you think happened?" Gilbert said.

"He never disappears."

"Couldn't he have gone to another town?" Agafon suggested.

"Not him," Vladimir said. "His life was in Auguliere. You had to know him the way I do. He's a ruthless man, but there are some redeeming qualities. If it weren't for him, there would be no Auguliere. Don't you see?"

"Maybe he's just inaccessible," Agafon said.

"He should have been in the village collecting taxes."

"I haven't seen him," Gilbert said.

"Neither has anyone. We'll go to the West End Slope to see if he is ill," Vladimir said.

The wagon bounced along the winding road, up the slope to the West End. Once the meadow opened, the wonderful carpet of green revealed the house. The chimney emitted no smoke. When they reached the house, the site they beheld shocked them. The house seemed oddly shifted to one side as though someone had pushed it. Vladimir was first to enter.

"Father!" he called, hearing his voice echo. "Father. Are you all right?" One wall was caved in like a small cart had driven through it. Gilbert looked down at the wood fragments.

"There are beetle grubs among the pieces. My cure never reached his house," Gilbert said.

They heard no sound nor movement in the house. They entered each room ready for anything. They heard squeaking from the boards on the floor above.

"Let's go upstairs," Gilbert said.

"He has rooms there." Vladimir said. The squeaking grew louder as they moved up. They saw a strange silhouette in the shadows. When they pressed closer, it moved back into the corner of the room. Gilbert entered the room first, seeking the creature hiding there. Suddenly it leapt past him, making hissing sounds.

"It's only his cat," Vladimir said. Agafon and Gilbert were relieved. They searched the other rooms until they came across a room containing belongings scattered all around inside. Scratch marks scarred the furniture and implements were strewn on the floor. In the middle of the bed they found what they had hoped they'd never find. Gilbert and Agafon looked at each other in disbelief. They both called, "Vladimir! Come here." Vladimir climbed the stairs until he arrived at the master bedroom and came in. To his horror there, on the bed he saw a skeleton in his father's clothes. "Agafon," Vladimir said, "You had better bring Madeleine."

"Madeleine?" Gilbert wondered.

"Sure."

"Take my wagon, Agafon," Gilbert said.

"Thanks," Agafon said. He ran outside, climbed up on the wagon, grabbed the reins and shouted, "Yaw!" to the horses and drove down the road, leaving a trail of dust.

Vladimir caught hold of Gilbert's arm, causing him to turn around. He beckoned him to sit on the floor with him. Once he commanded his attention, he looked at him with a more serious tone, ready to tell him something profound.

"I didn't tell you the whole truth," Vladimir said. "My dog was struck by a mule team, my father's mule team. He didn't mean to hit him. Chipper just ran out in front of the mules. My father tried to revive him. He wrapped his little paws, cleaned his wounds, and held him. Yet, with all his power, he couldn't save Chipper. It hurt very deeply. I don't blame my father. It was not his fault. If you could only look beyond his greed, there was a man underneath, a compassionate man. Now he's gone forever, just like that."

Agafon returned with Madeleine. When she saw the mangled body, she turned her head in disgust.

"I don't understand, Vladimir. Why does he have my father's medallion around his neck?"

"That's why I sent for you. He somehow got the idea in his head it belonged to him; that he was the rightful heir."

"He's not the heir of my father."

"Of course not. In his heart, Auguliere belonged to him and he extended that feeling to everyone and everything."

"Here's your father's medallion, Madeleine." Vladimir removed it from his father's neck and handed it to her. Madeleine knelt before him, taking the ornament with her two hands.

"So, Gilbert didn't take it," Madeleine said, repossessing the precious trophy.

"How could he?" Vladimir said. "Can't you see he's the redeemer of Auguliere?"

"I am so sorry, Gilbert." Gilbert bowed his head. Madeleine felt her heart tearing apart. The overwhelming emotions forced her to cry. She saw that Gilbert was touched by her feelings. She looked at him for forgiveness. Gilbert's kind face was receptive. She sensed his feelings at that moment better than she had ever sensed them before. Madeleine closed her eyes in relief, as Gilbert kissed her forehead.

"Gilbert," she said, looking up at him, "My father died three nights ago."

"That was the night of the full moon," Gilbert said.

"It was probably when my father was killed," Vladimir said.

"It was as though he knew . . ." Madeleine said.

"Yes," Gilbert assured, "he knew."

"He released you," Vladimir said. "Now you are free to leave Auguliere."

"No," Madeleine said, still sobbing. "Now I know Auguliere needs me more than ever." She turned her head to Gilbert. "I don't deserve you."

He wiped her tears away with his finger and looked at her directly, allowing a timid smile to flicker on his lips. During the time he looked at her face, she experienced the familiar feeling of well being which she knew before she withdrew her feelings from him.

"Everything will be fine," he reassured her.

"I am not the same person you knew when you came to Auguliere."

"You look the same to me."

"My exterior has not changed, but I am not the same inside."

"Why?"

"You opened my eyes. You enabled me to see things for the very first time. All my life, I wanted to see what lay on the other side of the mountain. When we were on the mountain, and you pointed out to me how the eagles soar, I felt like I was seeing them in a way I had never seen them before. I realized how truly free they were. It made me understand eagles exist there, too. People are the same no matter where you go."

"Yes, they are," Gilbert said.

"You also opened my heart. Your love of the world has taught me how to allow myself to have feelings and deal with them as an adult.

"I never realized I had so much of an effect on you."

"Finally, you taught me how to confront my fears. I learned to grow from them and to cope with the difficulties of life."

"I try to support what you want."

"You are a very strong man. Yes, in physical strength, but more importantly, in character."

"I think we have a lot of work to do in Auguliere," he said. She smiled back and nodded in agreement with him. She felt joined with him in a way she never knew before. She held his hand, rubbing the wet fingers in hers.

"You are the savior of Auguliere," Madeleine said.

"I am just a carpenter."

"No," Madeleine said fondly, reflecting on Vladimir. "It will be a new day in Auguliere."

"This village will need a new . . . 'landlord,'" Gilbert said. He looked up to Vladimir now with admiration.

"How will Auguliere be financed now without an official tax collector?"

"I was hoping you would say that," Vladimir said.

"Why?"

"Now I can tell you the real solution," Vladimir said, lowering his head. "I no longer have to fear reprimand." Vladimir stroked his beard protectively. "My father owned all the tea-bearing acreage in Auguliere. He provided the tea free of charge, at least in the beginning. He didn't believe a working man should have to buy tea, a basic necessity. He got greedy and realized he could sell it. I think greed single-handedly ruined his life or at least the spirit of it."

"How's that a solution?" Gilbert wondered.

"The one thing my father taught me was how to be a businessman," Vladimir said. "We can sell the tea, making it a much fairer way to collect revenue for the town. Believe me, there will be more than enough to run the town without any more taxes."

"Ah, yes!" Agafon said. "Tax relief. Now there's a democratic idea."

"If we are lucky, maybe, just maybe, we can reopen the zinc mines and be prosperous once more."

"We need to have a town hall meeting," Agafon said.

"I hereby nominate Vladimir Robertson as the new mayor of Auguliere," Madeleine said, never taking her eyes off Gilbert.

They heard the call of buzzards trying to discover the source of rotting flesh. The powerful horse odor seeped into the edifice. No one spoke. The four of them looked up at the ceiling of the decrepit house, as though to call upon a higher power.

Epilogue

This must have been the way it was a hundred years ago because today the Sayan Mountain range is home to one of the most famous resorts in Russia. Pioneers who ventured into the valley and probably made their home there centuries ago when life was simple founded the land. This has been a glimpse into the lives of these long forgotten, charming people in the annals of time, following many wars and political changes.

Iakov Knesnovich was probably one of those who lived in a valley like Auguliere. I remember the stories he told very well. He talked about their hardships, sacrifices and the greed of certain individuals who struggle for power. He spoke about how some people dealt with life's stresses; that some had to turn to alcohol to drown out life's misfortunes. There were the disappointments and the mistrusts that reigned supreme in a land that was once an island of hope in the middle of a vast wilderness, devoid of other beings. I remember each story, just the way they were told to me because *Iakov Knesnovich,* (or someone quite like him), was my grandfather.